A BEAUTIFUL STRUGGLE
The novel

Andrea Walker

ISBN-13:
978-1516900558

ISBN-10:
1516900553

DEDICATION

To
My Angel Face.
Jakaih Kierra, my first love.
And every Azhar around the world

Life Lesson's Build Strength and Life is Truly A Beautiful Struggle

-Andrea Walker

ACKNOWLEDGMENTS

To everyone who ever believed that I could do this,
and everyone who didn't, I appreciate you.

CHAPTER 1

"Azhar, I'm so proud of you. I always knew you would be my star child. I knew it since the day I laid eyes on you and the doctors gave me a choice of which day you were going to be born on since you were half in and half out as the clock struck midnight." Kat smoothed the stray strands of my bangs away from my eyes. Her fingertips noticeably burned made me cringe as they came close to my face.

"You have always been a force to be reckoned with."

"Mom, promise me you will go into the program tomorrow morning, first thing, please?"

"Oh Azhar, don't worry. I will go tomorrow morning, I promise. You just promise me that you will do good in school. Don't go there thinking you running stuff and no fighting! You hear me Azhar?"

"I'm not." I shifted my weight from one leg to the next hoping this wouldn't be some long drawn out conversation. I was anxious to get on the road and get to school.

"You don't be out there worrying about nothing back here. You go a head and live your life baby, no more worrying, you hear me?"

"No more worrying." I agreed. The words were barely audible because I wasn't quite convinced that I could live a life of no worries. I was already worried that Kat wouldn't make it to her drug rehab program the next morning if I wasn't there to literally take her. My mind was already worried that Rahiem and Kellie would actually be happy together and he would forget all about me. My mind worried about how I would survive off of two hundred and four dollars in cash and a hundred and twenty-six dollars in food stamps a month. I was already worried about having to possibly work and taking a full load of classes. Don't worry. Was there even a such thing?

My little Honda Accord was full to the brim with bins of clothes, my

1

little twenty-five inch TV and boxes of shoes for days.

"Baby girl, you go a head and continue to make your mom proud." It felt good to hear Kat say she was proud of me. Here I was about to be the first of my generation to attend college. She had missed my graduation and I had to hunt her down just to have her see me off to college. But in this moment I focused on the here and the now. Here, right now, I was hearing words that I longed to hear and creating moments that I had longed for. Over the years Kat had caused me so much pain and heartache, and though it was hard to refer to her as my mom to other people, I never called her anything other than mom to her face. Something inside me made me realize that she was due at least that much respect.

"Mom, I will be back in a few weeks after I get situated. I hope you are in the program by then and doing well. I know you can do this mom. Please, please mom do this one thing for me, this one time. Please?" I locked eyes with Kat. She darted her eyes to the ground.

"Come on Azhar. Don't do this to me right now. I said I was going to go. Don't put no guilt trips on me right now. I'm trying to be strong."

"Okay. I have to go." I knew that when I pressured Kat, she would run right to the first thing that was going to give her a high, so I eased out the conversation. I walked to my car and climbed in ready to start something new.

As I pulled out into traffic I looked into my rear view mirror. The distance between where Kat stood and I, grew further and further. Soon, I couldn't see her anymore. All I saw was the black road with the white line down the center. I turned the radio off and allowed my thoughts to drift back over my life.

I flipped through the mail that was neatly stacked on the dining room table. As usual, everything was addressed to Leigh, my cousin. Just as I was about to toss the envelopes aside, the last piece of mail caught my eye. 'Azhar Washington' it read. I tore it open and read my acceptance letter to Germantown High School, as if they needed to extend me a formal invitation. Where else would I be going since I didn't get accepted anywhere else? I flung the paper back down. It slid to the end of the deep mahogany table as I headed to my room.

"Just fucking great!" I said to myself half way up the stairs.

"What's just fucking great?" Leigh mimicked sarcastically, her enormous, hazel eyes piercing down at me. Her full-size lips were pressed tightly together displaying just how perfect they truly were. The new rouge-colored lipstick she wore simply intensified the obvious.

I hadn't even noticed Leigh standing at the top of the steps. My mind was running a million miles per second.

"Yeah, you betta watch that mouth of yours," Leigh hissed.

"Leigh, I gotta go to Germantown, man! Everybody goes there! That school ghetto as sh." The words were rolling off my tongue with no filter. I caught them just in time though.

"Well," Leigh was rummaging through her Chanel bag. "I bet next time you'll think about that when you're fooling around in school. Won't you?"

"But it's not my fault! If it wasn't for that damn Kat, then I would be just fine. I hate her!"

"What did I tell you about calling her Kat?" she shot at me. "That's your mother. Not Kat! At least give her that much respect Azhar!" Leigh passed me on the steps, not even turning to face me. I reach the top of the steps and walk toward my room. As I reach my bed, Leigh called out something about taking advantage of having a mother. That was one thing about Leigh; she never dogged Kat like everybody else in my family did. She was the only one who had any respect left for her.

"Azhar, you'll learn," Leigh yelled from downstairs, "You can't replace your mother. She'll always be your mother. No matter what, nobody can ever replace her."

"Whatever!" I mumbled flopping down on my bed and burying my head in my pillows. "I hate her!"

In life, nothing had ever been handed to me. I didn't inherit any money, accidentally find or win a million dollars, and I damn sure wasn't lucky enough to get a case that would leave me financially set for life. I mean, don't get me wrong, I didn't grow up in the projects, sleep five to a bed, live off of peanut butter and jelly, nor did I want for any materialistic item you could think of. But life for me, sure as hell wasn't some Huxtable sitcom.

I never liked to sugar coat shit, beat around the bush, and I'm damn sure not into punch–lines. So let me get straight to the point. For a long time I hated Kat, the woman who birthed me, until I realized that it was taking too much of my damn energy hating a woman who obviously hated herself. I actually felt sorry for her most days. Then there was Desmond, the man who forced Kat to have me, words cannot describe what I felt for him. Or maybe they can. The best one that came to mind was resentment.

I was told at an early age that Desmond was my father. He was a sorry excuse for a man, if you asked me. But if you let his family tell it, he was a hero, especially when I was a baby. "He saved your mom and sister," they would tell me. I guess they failed to realize, babies don't stay babies forever. I grew into beautiful young woman, filled with a bitter hate for adults who don't take responsibility for their own. All that shit his relatives said

Desmond used to do for me they can save for the birds. Desmond Edward Washington was not and will never be my father!

Let me clear something up before we go any further, I don't hate Desmond. I don't even wish anything bad on him. It's more like what Tupac said "My anger wouldn't let me feel for a stranger."

See, the way I see it is, I wasn't a child brought into this world out of love. I was a child forced into this world out of hate and revenge. My mother, Kat, was just twenty-one and already had my older sister, Cashay, who was four at the time. It was the early 80's and crack had hit Richard Allen projects big-time. Desmond was supposed to be this all-out, hard-working man who supported my mother and my sister. A college man, I was told. Headed for big things, I suppose. But according to Kat, in the midst of all these great things that Desmond was supposed to be, he was also an alcoholic and did a little crack here and there. Kat told me that before she knew it, she and Desmond only got along when they both were bent.

I, Azhar Faith Washington am the aftermath of a gunshot gone horribly wrong, or right if you're an optimistic person like my Aunt Debbie always tells me to be. According to Kat, she was hosting a small gathering for Desmond's birthday, the kind of party with eight or nine kids running in and out the small apartment on the ground floor, while all the adults sat around drinking, smoking, and cursing.

"The radio was blasting Kool and the Gang," said Kat. "Incense was burning, laughter and high-pitched voices filled the air, and all of your Aunts were there with their men of the hour, and a few other neighbors. The place was jam-packed." She even admitted that the tables were covered with adult party favors: playing cards, big bottles of Olde English and Taylor's Port, Newports, lighters, Top paper, thick bags of reefa, a couple of crack pipes, some razor blades and a few small mirrors lined with a white powdery substance.

"Next thing I know, my back was firmly pressed against the closet door," Kat told me. "My skirt was hiked up around my waist and your Uncle Damien was dominating my movements." From pictures, I remember that my Uncle towered over her, and pictured him vigorously squeezing her perky C cups, sucking and biting her lips in between pants while his right hand held onto her firm ass.

Kat told me her inner demons tussled vigorously, influenced by drugs, then she gave into Damien's hands guiding her to her knees. She lowered herself to the floor and as if on cue, Desmond appeared in the doorway of the room, and she froze.

"The music was still blaring, but all I heard was the rapid thumping in my chest." Then Kat described Uncle Damien casually sliding his penis back in his pants and smirking, letting out a soft chuckle. "That's all it took.

Desmond charged at your Uncle, they fought, my head was spinning, and next thing I knew the sound of the gun exploded in the air, echoing passed my eardrum."

My Uncle Damien was pronounced dead on arrival November 11, 1982 at 7:42pm at Temple University Hospital.

That February, Kat found out she was pregnant with me. She said she had no doubt in her mind what she would do about her situation–get an abortion. But Desmond wouldn't have it.

"Kitty, you will not kill my child! Forso help me God, I will kill you first," Is how Kat quoted him.

"And I told him, 'Desmond this is my body and I don't want this baby' but we know how that turned out." Kat told me all of this as if I wasn't the unwanted baby in question.

Desmond shook his head, Kat said, "He knew I was one headstrong female. He knew he couldn't force me to do anything I didn't want to do. And he knew the only way he could get me to keep you was by force." Kat's voice begins to rise, "He had to get his family involved."

And then one morning in late march, all of my Aunts cornered Kat and intimidated her into keeping me.

"You, you owe me this life," is what Desmond told her. "Kitty, you owe all of us this life," added my Aunt Charlene. "We are all family here. We are all you have and now you owe us this life for Damien."

Katherine, Kitty, Kat. Three uniquely, different women. Though I only knew Kat, they all were my mother. Kat told me that Katherine died the day Mr. George climbed on top of her and "ripped me wide open!" She told me every detail of that day she felt like someone "gutted" her like a fish. She said from that day forward she always felt empty and numb. Kat said that once someone takes you the way Mr. George took her, you become someone else. I fought back tears as the images of the big black man with the salt and pepper beard and balding head raised my mother's eight-year-old skinny little legs above her head. Kat seemed unbothered. Her facial expression was still soft as the words escaped her lips. She told the story, never making eye contact with me until she got to the part where she said, "baby girl, you possess a power so great, that men will pay anything, do anything, just to have you. You control the way a man will treat you." Her eyes locked firmly with mine, and it was then that I realized that Kat was more than some dirty junkie like my family insinuated. I felt something strong from her during these sporadic life lesson talks we would have. She was strong.

Kat said that Kitty died when she was gang rapped one cold night in the streets of Michigan. She told me how out of nowhere she grabbed a glass bottle and bashed her attacker in the head and began viciously stabbing him in the neck and head with the remaining piece of glass in her hand. "You have to be strong Azhar, you can't let anyone take you if you don't want to give them their way. Nobody, owns you. You are your own keeper." The emphasis put on her last words always rang out in my head. I am my own keeper. I asked Kat if she cried when this was happening and she said "Cry for what? That wasn't gonna make him stop taking me. Mr. George didn't stop taking me no matter how much I cried. And my momma didn't believe me no matter how many times I cried and begged her to. Tears mean nothing Azhar! They just show how scared and weak you really are, and once a person knows you're scared and weak." She looked at me intensely, taking my chin into her hands, raising it on a tilt so that our eyes came to meet. "once they know that, they got you and they will use that against you every chance they get. You have to be fearless."

Sometimes I wondered if Mr. George didn't rape my mom, if Katherine would have been a good mom to me and my sister. I wondered if Katherine would have chose to live a life of prostitution and drug using. Everyday I wondered if Katherine would have been HIV positive. Mr. George not only ruined my mother's life, but he ruined mines too, and Chas's. He not only raped my mother but he raped me of my childhood and of any hope of ever having a normal family. I hated Mr. George and anyone who bore any resemblance to the man in the black and white photos my mother showed me of him.

For nine long months, Kat carried an unwanted child. She told me this when I was just twelve years old. Kat always said I was wise beyond my years and that talking to me, even at just twelve years old, was like talking to a twenty two year old. Kat held so much guilt in her heart for the death of Damien, she felt having me was the only way she could repay Desmond and his family. Throughout those months, Kat tried hard not to subject me to the white powdery substance she indulged in so heavily while pregnant with Cashay. But it seemed almost impossible for her to avoid it since her apartment was the family's hang out spot. Every Friday, when somebody got paid, there was a party. Kat's nights were the longest. She often stayed in her room, alone, staring at the small black and white TV while listening to everyone downstairs curse, laugh and carry on. The parties lasted until morning, and sometimes until it was time for Kat to take Cash to school. In the later part of Kat's pregnancy, her resistance weakened and she found herself downstairs slightly sipping on a drink. Sometimes if she was "good" Desmond would allow her to snort a line or two or take a few puffs of the pipe. But two lines were her max, she once told me.

While she was pregnant she agreed she wouldn't shoot up and Desmond always reminded her of her agreement during the parties. He would pull her in the kitchen and rub her belly. "I know you miss this good stuff and everything, but soon this will be over and you can have whatever you want. Just give me a healthy handsome son."

My oversized, walnut eyes opened on October 31, 1983, "the devil's birthday," my grandmother Azell once said to me. All twelve of Desmond's sisters and brothers stood proudly by as my mother delivered me via cesarean section, into hell on earth.

I went home from the hospital with Kat and Desmond but, by the time I turned four, I was living with my Big Mom, my mother's grandmother and my mom's older sister, Bobbie. Desmond hasn't done a damn thing for me since I was four, other than fuel my anger whenever we cross paths.

Dear Diary,

When I look at him, I don't see me.

Not even a small little glimpse.

And I search my brain for the answer as to who you really are.

Then, it comes to me.

I remember.

They said that you, the man who never attended one out of twenty-one of my birthdays, a man who has never seen one out of three of my graduations, the man that only showed up every three years, who only stuck around for a day or two and only bought me presents on holidays, if you were not in jail then.

You're the man who killed his brother and forced my mother to carry me, your child.

The man who held the gun to her head and threatened to blow her brains out.

You're the man that they all brag about but, when I look at you, I see none of what they see.

I try hard to look at you and see the man that they say you used to be.

But I don't.

I can't.

Too much time has passed and too many promises broken; too many lies told, and too many questions unanswered.

I wish that I could turn back the hands of time and be that little girl with the shiny shoes and lace stockings.

And you?

You would be my night and shining armor.

But I can't.

I won't.

I won't allow you to fool me like you fooled them.

I just want to know how could you?

Lie to me?

Not love me?

Not want me?

Not need me?

Not except me?

Not show me...

How to ride a bike, tie my shoe, or tell me not to do all the fast things little girls aren't supposed to do?

Did you know that I graduated elementary, middle, high school and soon college?

Did you know that, at seventeen, I carried a child for eight weeks and four days?

I sat and wondered if I would have been in that predicament if only I had a dad to love me, instead of thinking that I needed love, which only came in the form of sex?

Did you know that you were absent from my life for so long that…

I sometimes forget that you even exist?

I don't know you.

All I know is that your last name is the same as mine; and that you, me, and my mom share the same sign.

My childhood memories of you consist of you living directly across the street from me and never bothering to come and see me.

I remember seeing you go in and out of that house.

The one that everyone knew was the crack house.

I remember you living in that house with my friend's mother, who was my mother's best friend.

You broke Kat's heart.

I remember you sneaking in and out, and not coming out at all if I were sitting on my steps watching that door for you to appear.

But it was always just as I turned to go in, that you would slip out and go running down the street.

That broke my heart.

Some days I think you would even sneak out the backdoor.

All I knew is that you couldn't have loved me.

I remember not understanding why you were over there with her and her daughter, who was my friend, but wouldn't even call me.

I remember the summer that you decided that you wanted to make things right and you took me to see the fireworks.

I was all excited, until my friend came knocking on my door with her mother, who was my mother's best friend, in toe.

The one who everyone knew was a crackhead.

Not that my mom wasn't, but why'd you have to live over there and be her dad and not mine?

You carried her daughter on your neck, like you did me sometimes, but not that night.

You held her mother's hand and carried her on your neck.

My feet were hurting so badly, they had blisters the next day from all the walking we did that night.

I cried the whole way home for my mommy, who I hadn't seen in what seemed like forever, but that didn't matter.

I loved her.

She could do no wrong in my eyes; but you?

You are different.

You are a man.

And they told me how you were the one who introduced those drugs to my mother.
Why?
I've tried so hard to rid myself of this feeling for you.
But I'm not sure I've got enough strength in me.
You forced me into hell and the only way out is death.
And I'm scared of that.
Some days are better than others, but none as good as never being here.
I'm sorry that I hate you and I can't tell you to your face.
I want you continue to see me as this strong woman that grew so beautifully inside and out without you.

Me admitting that you've had such drastic effects on my life would lead you to believe that I care about you and I don't cause...

My anger will not let me feel for a stranger.

CHAPTER 2

My mother was born Katherine T. Young on November 1, 1962, to William James Young and Gina Loraine Jefferson. William was shot dead in front of Kat when she was just two years old by my Grandma Gina's new boyfriend, Mr. George. Mr. George was never convicted of the murder though and my grandmother stayed with him.

Kat told me that my grandmother was a beautiful, thin, loud and audacious woman with a white mother and black father. Her mother's features were more dominant, giving her soft pale skin and bright-grey eyes, like diamonds. She had thin lips and a small thin nose. Her hair hung down her back to her behind. She was a beauty and it seemed every man wanted her.

My Grandma Gina gave birth to six children, including Kat, but raised none of them. She drank heavily from a very young age and died of lung cancer in her late forties. Her mother, my Big Mom, raised all of Gina's children. I never recall meeting Gina, just seeing the pictures.

Kat had a smooth, coco-colored complexion skin, with pretty, long, jet-black hair. Her eyes were large and filled most of her face, something I inherited from her. Kat's father, William was Native American and his traits ran strong. Kat had dimples in both of her cheeks and a distinguished, yet, flat mole above her lip on the right side of her face. She stood 5'3" and weighed around one hundred fifteen pounds.

I was five years old when I noticed how beautiful my mother was. It was the same day I watched my family beat her down like she was a stranger in the street. I had spent the weekend with my Aunt Debbie, Kat's older sister. Kat and I were walking back home. The night was cool and breezy. Filling my nostrils, I inhaled the smell of summer, walking up the steps to the porch with my mom. In my right hand I held a small, clear glass jar filled with jellybeans of all colors. My left hand gripped the black iron railing on the steps. Suddenly, my Aunt Bobbie and her two daughters, Crystal and

Christina rushed out of the house. Big Mom was still alive at that time. She grabbed me by the hand and snatched me in the house. I tried to pull away from her grip as I caught sight of the horrid look on my mother's face. I heard loud thumping noises as my mom screamed for help.

"Please, somebody help me! I'm pregnant!" She cried out over and over again.

Once inside I ran to the window. My Aunt Bobbie was standing over Kat with a wooden baseball bat while, Christina, her oldest daughter, kicked and stomped. I watched helplessly, tears streaming from my eyes. A few minutes later my Aunt Bobbie and her daughters came in the house. Kat lay on the porch in fetal position crying, and gasping while holding her stomach. That was the first of many beatings Kat took from the family. Kat's drug habit often forced her to steal from us. She would take leather coats on her occasional visits, money, or anything of value that was laying around. My Aunt Bobbie even thought that Cash and I were letting Kat in the house when nobody was home, but we weren't. She still beat us for it anyway.

Around this time I began feeling distant and unloved, as if I just didn't fit in. I was only five years old but I knew what they had done to Kat wasn't right. I had a love for Kat that she didn't quite reciprocate, but I knew I felt something from her. With my Aunt Bobbie and her daughters, I felt nothing. And when my Big Mom died, I felt extremely out of place; like a stranger in my own home.

Kat would be gone from my life for years at a time. My birthday, Christmas and Mother's Day would come and go, but still no Kat. When she would stop by, I'm guessing to steal whatever was in eyesight, she would sit me down and promise me that she would be right back or that she was out looking for us a house, so that we could be a real family. Those lies quickly got old. As I got older she would just say, "I'll be back, I promise." One thing that I remember Desmond told me when I was seven was that promises were made to be broken. So I always knew that my mother was lying even though I hoped and prayed that she wasn't.

On a humid summer afternoon Cash and I walked down our block eating our twenty-five cent Big popsicles. The blue dye had stained my fingers but I didn't care, I was just happy for the temporary cool relief it provided. The sun was beating on my freshly braided hair and felt like it was burning holes in my scalp from all the grease my cousin Crystal used. I couldn't wait to reach our front door.

"Race you!" Cash said as we approached our house. She took off running before her words fully landed.

"Cheater!" I called after her trying to catch up. Her extra long legs provided her an advantage, and she reached the steps, taking them two at a time, long before I got there. When I finally hit the top step, not looking, I ran right into the back of Cash, who was frozen in the doorway. My eyes darted around the side of her to see inside the house. Kat. It was Kat. I should have known. It was always her. She was the center of our lives, the creator of much confusion, chaos, and emotional torment even though she was more absent than present.

The look of anguish and sadness disappeared as soon as she saw us. Kat's eyes bounced in delight back and forth from me to Cash. She sprinted to her feet. Cash and I stood still. I could tell we both were feeling the same thing, confused. Our desire for a mother fought our resentment from abandonment and rejection divided us.

"Babies!" She stretched her arms out, welcoming us into them. My emotions ran crazy. Deep in the pit of the stomach I felt it knotting up, the lump in my throat rising. I didn't know if I was going to cry or jump for joy. I quickly erased that thought of joy. Kat wasn't going to stay. She never stayed and she never took us with her.

Her stench was the same as always. A mix of sweet perfume and dirty clothes. Her fingertips were black, her nails chipped and filthy. Despite all this, her smile lit up the room. Her energy was forcing happiness into Cash and I. I tried to fight it but I couldn't.

"Come sit down babies. Sit here next to mommy." Kat patted the couch.

I looked to my Aunt Bobbie for confirmation. Her face was strained. Something was wrong. My Aunt Debbie sat with her legs crossed, so poised. She held a tissue in her hand that she kept patting her forehead with.

"We want to talk to you about something really important."

My heart raced as the words escaped Kat's mouth. I could see her lips moving but the only words I understood were "mommy is sick." Somewhere in between her sobs she said the letters "HIV" and then she began to cry uncontrollably. Everybody sat motionless. I faded out of the conversation, retreating into my own mind until my Aunt Bobbie dismissed us from the conversation with a "Y'all go head upstairs to your room while we talk with your mom."

Kat left that evening after telling us that she had HIV. We didn't see her for a long time after that again. Life went back to normal. The beatings, my Aunt's late night grown folks parties, the lonely days of being home alone, the longing for Kat, the yearning for the understanding of this thing called life.

I breathed a sigh of relief every day that passed without me or my sister catching a beat down. But those days were few and far in-between. In my Aunt Bobbie's eyes, it never mattered if we were being good or not, it was as if there was always something for her to complain about, and ultimately beat us for. Some days it would be for things like not putting our dirty clothes in the bag the night before or not making our beds properly.

Other times, Cash would forget to push the chairs in under tables or not take out the trash. Cash had a lot of chores and I'm not sure if she really forgot sometimes or she really just didn't care, but I swear every time she got a beating it was like I got one, too. Listening to her, having to hear her scream and see her skin being snatched off her body with the extension cord or the broom or a thorny branch from the rose tree bush, made me hold my breath and pray to God that it would be over soon.

I knew that I couldn't spend my entire life there. I began conjuring up a plan to move in with my Aunt Debbie. I just had to convince my Aunt Bobbie to let me move. It was so much easier said than done. The fact that I was totally terrified of my Aunt Bobbie made this little plan even more difficult to execute. The mere thought of having to say anything other than my daily two words, "good morning," even made me feel queasy. I didn't know it then but, like my mother, my Aunt Bobbie was a drug addict. I assume, now, that the hell she put me and Cash through as children was a result of her mood swings when she was either high or going through a withdrawal.

When I was about nine years old, things started getting worse at home between Cash and Aunt Bobbie. Cash's dumb ass went and got pregnant. Cash and I were not close, even though we shared a room and the same bed for about nine years. We weren't anything alike, total opposites in features and personality. The one thing we did have in common was being unhappy about living with Aunt Bobbie.

Cash was extremely withdrawn and quiet as I was too but her's was in a very unpleasant way. I couldn't figure out for the life of me why she was so damn weird. I kind of sensed at a young age that Cash and I were different. Yes, we came by way of the same birth canal; shared the same horrible abuse, mentally and physically, but Cash was not totally with it, mentally, I mean. Once I got to be about eight or nine years old I realized that the word LD that my Aunt Bobbie used so carelessly when describing Cash stood for learning disability. Although Cash and I attended the same school, I thought that Cash's class only consisted of five people because she was advanced as I was in math and reading. I guess my young mind couldn't quite distinguish between the two, or perhaps I really didn't care at all to even ask. I just knew that I was placed in advanced reading and math in kindergarten because my Aunt would drill my numbers into my head all day long for hours. I would have to read two chapter books a week, and on Saturdays I had spelling words and book reports. Even my summers were filled with math test, spelling bees and three and four page book reports. I would sit at the kitchen table for three or four hours some days, just practicing my handwriting. All of this began when I was five years old and as I got older, the work got more intense and more demanding. I was placed in the mentally gifted program when I entered the fourth grade. Times tables were like hell to me. I think my Aunt loved to watch me get all worked up. I could do whatever work she gave me as long as I was alone without her staring down my throat. But, when it came to my times table, she would sit right in front of me, running off numbers, impatiently waiting on a speedy answer. "Eight times eight?" She would probe.

"Sixty four."

"Seven times twelve is?" she spat faster.

"Eighty four."

"Six times fourteen?"

"Eighty four." I hurriedly said uneasy.

"Sixteen times eight?"

I'd start counting on my fingers nervously. Thinking to myself who the hell would know that? "Ahhh, a hundred and eighteen, I mean twenty ah."

"Go back and start from your two times tables. I want them all written two times each, up to your twenty times tables." This would go on for days, not as a punishment but, just because I think my Aunt Bobbie didn't think kids were supposed to have fun. My time outside was limited because I had a bedtime of eight o'clock, even once I reached the fifth grade. I'd sometimes be doing homework until that hour and then have to rush and eat dinner and then straight to bed. My Aunt Bobbie had a rule that no one was to go outside until their homework was perfect, checked and signed off by either her or one of her two daughters. So that meant that even if she didn't come home until seven thirty that night, we were not to even step foot on the porch. I spent most of my days confined to my room playing Barbie's, reading and writing by myself while Cash was down stairs sneaking to watch music videos, which we were forbid to do.

Cash distanced herself from me. I think partially because Aunt Bobbie often compared us to one another even though we were five years apart. Cash didn't like it when Aunt Bobbie would keep reminding her of something I could do that she couldn't, which made her not like me.

Cash's pregnancy didn't last long though. Aunt Bobbie beat her up in the abortion clinic because Cash wouldn't sign the papers to allow the procedure, and she lost the baby two weeks later. That's when Cash ran away. She didn't sneak out the window or leave late at night like people did in the movies or anything. She just walked out the front door crying. I ran after her crying, too. She couldn't leave me there in that house all by myself. *Was she crazy? I'd die*, I thought. Cash was forever catching all the gruesome beatings; the ones that lasted for twenty minutes or more with hangers, belt buckles, and extension cords and I feared that kind of treatment if she left me there alone.

"Cash, please don't leave me here, please," I begged.

She hugged me tight. "I'll be back for you," she said, showing me affection for the first time.

"You promise?" I yelled after her.

She stopped and nodded her head.

I ran down the steps after her. "Please don't go, Cash, please. I'm begging you, please."

But she kept on walking faster and faster down the street. Once I could no longer see her, I got scared because that meant that she was headed outside of the box. The box consisted of a six block radius. Inside that box was our home, our school, the lottery place and the market. The only places we were able to walk to. Lord knows we rarely stepped outside of the box. I couldn't tell you left from right once we left the box. I wondered where Cash would go. I tried to put myself in her shoes but I'd probably end up walking right back up that block unable to go anywhere else, because 2010 Crowley Street was all I knew.

After Cash ran away that day, she was placed in DHS. That was the last I'd seen Cash until I was fourteen years old. I guess she thought Kat would come and rescue her ass like she did before. At that time I was in the first grade or so and Aunt Bobbie had beat the holy shit out of Cash with this big brown extension cord. I was down stairs packing my school bag up when my Aunt Bobbie came home. The night before she had called and told Cash to make sure she cleaned the kitchen before going to bed and I don't know why but, Cash didn't and for that, Cash was destined to catch it. I sat on the edge of the couch, clutching my fingers tightly together, praying that God came and made my Aunt stop whipping on Cash the way she was. I could hear the cord slapping wildly across Cash's bare skin. "Please, Aunt Bobbie, please, I'm sorry!" Cash screamed in between hits of the cord.

"When I tell yah stupid ass to do something, you fucking do it." My Aunt responded.

"I'm sorry, please! I can't breathe, please, I'm bleeding!" Cash continued to scream but that extension cord did not stop slapping her skin. It seemed to pick up speed with each passing hit.

"Oh you wanna run, huh, you gone make me chase yah stupid ass?" my Aunt Bobbie yelled out. When I heard her coming down those steps I ran into the kitchen to get as far away from her as possible. I saw her grab her old broomstick from behind the front door and head back up the stairs to finish with Cash.

"Please, God, help Cash. Please, Lord, take the pain and protect Cash." I prayed and began crying just at the thought of what was about to happen now.

"Help, help me somebody help me." Cash now cried out. Her cries were now screams for dear life.

"Please help!" I felt helpless and nauseas. Where was the Lord when I most needed Him? After another what seemed like twenty minutes, when I could no longer hear Cash cry, my Aunt Bobbie came walking down the steps. I sat under the dining room table hiding like I did when I was scared and wanted to disappear. I snuck up the stairs and found Cash barely alive it looked like. Her body was so swelled up. Her eyes were swollen nearly shut. Cash was supposed to be graduating the next day. That morning when we left for school, Cash could barely walk. Her wrist was bulging and clearly broke or something. Her face was severely bruised and swollen and her eye turning dark blue-green. She cried the entire walk to school, which was a very long one this day. She begged me all the way to school to come with her to the office and report it to the principal. I was too scared though. All I could think about was the beating that we would get if Aunt Bobbie found out that we were telling people what she was doing to us. I couldn't bear the thought of how bad that one would hurt. I didn't think I would be able to live through that kind of beating that we would surely get. I left Cash. I ran straight to class and kept my mouth shut all day. I blacked out all that had happened that morning and focused on my work in school.

After school, we walked home as usual and I felt sorry for Cash because I knew that the school would have to call Aunt Bobbie and tell her what Cash had did. As we walked up the bottom of the block, we saw three police cars and whole lot of people surrounding our house. My feet froze; they wouldn't let me move. My heart dropped into my hands. Lord, what the hell did Cash do now? Tears began to form because all I knew was that I didn't want to end up in foster care. My Aunt Bobbie had always told us that if we didn't live with her, then DHS was the only alternative. She would threaten us all the time when we didn't do as we were told. "You know what," she would say, "I'll just take y'all stupid asses to DHS. See how y'all like that." I didn't know what DHS was but from the sounds of things, it was pretty bad. I guessed it was a jail or something for unwanted little kids. I wanted to be wanted more than anything. I wanted Kat to want me.

Finally, Cash pulled me up the street by my hand. We reached the steps and there was Kat in tears screaming at my Aunt Bobbie. My Aunt Debbie was trying to calm her down and the police were asking our neighbors questions. When they noticed us standing there, they all came over to us.

There was a person from DHS, family service and so on. Cash showed them her bruises, cuts, scrapes, and scars from that morning. She told them everything. I just sat there, quietly. I prayed and cried inside as I watched all the commotion going on. I prayed that I would wake up from this horrible dream that I called my life. I asked God why this had to be *my* life and not someone else's. But, as I sat there praying, I realized that I had been asking these same questions since my Big Mom was alive and had taught me about the Lord. I seemed to always have the same question.

I don't know what happened to my Aunt Bobbie. All I know was that we went to live with Kat in her three-bedroom apartment with her boyfriend for the summer.

Here we were, finally living with Kat, and when she was around and not high, I loved her and everything about her. She was funny and had this glow about her. She was witty and a bit sassy. I know now that's where I inherited all those traits from. The good thing was that Kat lived two blocks from Aunt Debbie so we spent most of our days up the street at her house. It was during these summer days that Nikki, my Aunt Debbie's youngest daughter and I began forming our sister-bond.

This was probably the best summer I ever had. We spent hours playing in the fire hydrant that Uncle Tony would turn on everyday for us. We sat on the steps cooling off when the sun would begin going down, eating cheese pretzels and cherry water ice. Hopscotch and jump rope tired our legs out but not before we played hide and go seek or freeze tag. I was the youngest of all the cousins, the baby they would remind me. I always ended up being it and aimlessly running behind everyone trying to keep up.

Summer ended and back to Aunt Bobbie's house we went. I guess she just needed a break or something. That was the only time I can remember living with Kat and enjoying it. That was also the only time I can recall Kat being clean longer than three days. Still in all, at that point in my life, I hadn't a clue as to what drugs were. All I knew was that Kat loved and adored being and doing whatever it was that she did in the streets more than being with me. I can recall waking up many of nights that summer to an empty apartment, just Cash and I. Daylight would come knocking and Kat would eventually come stumbling through the door. Her eyes would be bucked wide open and blood shot red. Her fingers were always burned and dirty, and the icing on the cake would be her uncontrollable stuttering along with the flickering of her tongue. The day Cash ran away, I guess she was hoping for Kat to come and be her hero like she did that one summer. Kat never came though.

CHAPTER 3

The summer after Cash ran away I turned eleven and I moved in with my Aunt Debbie, my Uncle Tony and their youngest daughter Nikki. I guess my Aunt Bobbie finally just said fuck it and let me go, since I had been spending the past three summers and every weekend at my Aunt Debbie's house.

Debra Jones was my mother's older sister. The only one out of six of my grandmother Gina's children who made it out of the drug era in one piece with most of her sanity. My Aunt was a very poised woman, fair skinned with long jet-black hair. She took pride in her looks and her possessions. She would take at least two hours to get dressed everyday no matter where she was going, grocery store included. She was always reminding us of the things that were expected of a woman and how important our hygiene was. My Aunt was soft spoken and never yelled, swore or beat us.

My Uncle Tony was a ladies' man. Tall, dark and handsome, my Aunt would refer to him as with sarcasm in her voice. Uncle Tony was about 6'3", thin build and never seemed to age. His voice was deep and stern. It sent chills down my back when he would speak to me. Though my Uncle Tony wasn't abusive like my Aunt Bobbie, his voice alone told me he would tear fire to my ass if I got out line, so I didn't.

But there was this one time that I got all dramatic like I was going to overdose on Tylenol because I had to go back home to my Aunt Bobbie's house. The weekend had come to an end and just like every time it was time for me to go back to Aunt Bobbie's house, I got all flustered and anxiety took over and I began doing my begging and pleading and carrying on so much that I began to get a headache. Aunt Debbie told me to take a Tylenol and that I would be okay. I had remembered reading a book I had found at Aunt Bobbie's house called *Girl Interrupted* by Susanna Kaysen where a girl had attempted suicide by overdosing on pills. She was committed to a mental institute though. I don't know what I was thinking or if I was thinking this all the way through at all. I do remember thinking that maybe if my Aunt and Uncle saw just had paranoid I was to return to Aunt Bobbie's house they would let me stay. Instead, Uncle Tony came strolling in the front room where I lay across the bed holding the medicine bottle in my hand. He snatched the bottle and gripped me up by my arms off the bed like a rag doll and shook me so effortlessly.

"You wanna die?! You tryna kill yourself? You want me to help you? Huh?" I was so scared I could feel tinkles of pee escaping me. I held my breath hoping to pass out to avoid this beating I surely was about to get. A few moments of silence while being held in the air by my arms and my Uncle pulled me close to him and gave me a big hug. It was the first time I had ever seen my Uncle in a vulnerable state. He was always so well poised in his stern outer shell which mimicked my Aunt Debbie's. No hugs, no kisses, no mushy mushy stuff like they did on Full House or the After School Specials.

My Aunt Debbie and Uncle Tony had three kids. There was lil' Tony, their oldest daughter AshLeigh who we all called Leigh and then there was Nikki whose real name was Nigera.

Nikki and I were only two years apart. We had been calling each other sisters since I could remember and did everything together, just like sisters. If Nikki liked pink, I liked pink too. If Nikki wanted to do dance or cheerleading, I was right there with her. Nikki had this confidence about her that said *Don't fuck with me, bitch*! I loved her swag, even at only eleven years old. Nikki was truly my Aunt's child. Her fair skin and thick, shoulder length, black hair was always neatly styled and she was big on her hygiene as well. That summer, Nikki and I got into cheerleading, dance and girl scouts. There were no more summers spent at the kitchen table for me. We took trips to all the amusement parks and went to camp and flea markets and even went swimming at local pools. I didn't completely escape my Aunt Bobbie though. Every now and then, my Aunt Debbie would need a break and send Nikki and I over there for a few days, but those days were nothing like they used to be. We were allowed outside and could stay up late and watch TV, too.

This was the life I thought I should have been living. I was so happy; I even started writing Jones at the end of my name. The Jones' were my family and I loved it. Everything was good. That's why when Kat came back into my life, all I could do was rebel. It was the middle of my eighth grade year.

She popped up one day out of the clear blue, demanding that I come and live with her. It was at this point in my life where I felt she no longer deserved the title "mom" from me. She became Kat, and at first everyone was opposed to me calling her Kat but really, what could my Aunt Debbie really say? She referred to her own mother as Gina.

I finally understood what was meant by "be careful for what you wish for." I had wished and prayed for my mother for as long as I could remember, and here it was, but no longer did I want Kat. After many sleepless nights at my Aunt Bobbie's, I sometimes wished Kat would die. When she was missing in action for months or years at a time, I would pray that God hurried up and took her away so that I didn't have to worry anymore, because she would be in a better place. I don't know if the hate in me just wanted her to die, or if the pain in me from worrying just wanted better for her and me.

Maybe some of it was the stories I had heard about over the years. Like the one where she sold me for drugs when I was two years old, or the one where she left me in a crack house for days and forgot about me. Or the time she allowed me to get so filthy that I caught lice in my hair and eyebrows and had to have it cut out. I began to think I was adopted or switched at birth. Something, anything; Kat couldn't be my mother. What kind of person does all of these things to a child well before the child even turns five years old?

I was devastated that Wednesday afternoon when I came home from school and found my stuff all packed up. I hadn't seen Kat for almost two years. The last time was the day everyone kept talking about HIV.

Kat took me to Michigan where she lived. I not only hated Kat at this point, but I feared her too. She didn't look or act sick but the word HIV had been something that I had began to hear more and more about. In school we had a guest speaker come and talk about HIV and AIDS. He said that it could be contracted through spit and that they were still studying the effects of contracting it through sweat. The man talked a lot that day but I listened in spurts dipping in and out of my own thoughts. When he said it was sexually transmitted I began to wonder who had given it to Kat. I immediately thought about Desmond and my Uncle Damien. My mind raced even more at the thought of who my little brother Shawn's dad was. Had Shawn's dad given Kat HIV? Did Shawn have HIV? Did Desmond or my Uncle Damien give Kat HIV? Did I have HIV? Panic flooded me my entire stay in Michigan. Kat caused too many thoughts and questions that my little thirteen year old brain was not quite equipped to handle. When she was gone from my life, I didn't have to deal with her or her sickness or the possibility of me being sick with HIV. When she was gone, she was dead to me, and anyone who didn't already know me thought that my Aunt Debbie was my mom. Nobody spoke about Kat or her HIV while she was doing her disappearing acts.

It was just another day without school for me when Kat walked in with one of her many male friends. Her boyfriend was usually there, but this was one of the days he decided to go look for a job. I hadn't been out of the small efficiency apartment in about four days. That had been the last time I had spoke with my Aunt Debbie. I had begged her to come and get me. I cried, screamed and even prayed on the phone with her. But she said that there was nothing she could do, that there were a lot of things she was handling at home at that time with my Uncle Tony. I felt like the walls around me were closing in on me. My heart raced for hours nonstop. I felt helpless. That evening, I curled up on the small sofa and stayed there.

Kat walked in with a small brown paper bag. She didn't even bother to introduce me to her male friend. Not that I cared for his name. I knew it would be a cold day in hell before I would see him again. Every few months Kat had a new man whom she was about to be married to. And within weeks or days these men would just mysteriously fade into thin air, no explanation or anything.

Kat walked in the bathroom swiftly and back out the door just as quickly not even looking in my direction. The sun set just as I was about to watch the six o'clock news. Just then, I felt my little stomach remind me that I hadn't eaten all day. I cracked the refrigerator hoping for a quick peanut butter and jelly or tuna fish sandwich. But as I suspected the only thing that the refrigerator held was some leftover spaghetti, a half-gallon of two percent milk, a jar of mayonnaise, some other condiments, and three slices of bread. The cabinets held four cans of pinto beans, a can of sliced carrots, a box of vanilla pudding and one pack of grape Kool-Aid. The freezer held only a tray of ice and a half-gallon of freezer burnt chocolate chip ice cream. I decided to make do with the pudding; that was until I poured the milk into it. The smell almost knocked me out, not to mention the logs that came falling out of it. I next decided on the spaghetti. Though I had to pick around some parts of it that had started to mildew, it was either that or sliced carrots. The night came fast and before you knew it the clock on the nightstand next to my mother's bed read 12:45 am. The next morning, my mother's boyfriend, Kevin, awakened me. He said good morning and looked in the bathroom, I guess, expecting to see my mother. But, to his surprise, she was not there.

"She ain't here." I said turning over to my side. He seemed really surprised. I guess it was only me that Kat couldn't fool.

"Well, where she at?" he said rubbing his almost balding head.

"I don't know; she left yesterday morning."

Kevin looked in the refrigerator and smiled. I don't know what the hell he was smiling at, cause that shit wasn't the least bit of funny to me. He looked at me again rubbing his head. He let out a long sigh and then said,

"I'll be right back."

I don't know what "be right back" meant to him was, but two days later I heard a loud knock on the door and someone calling my name. It was my Aunt Debbie. I jumped up and snatched opened the door, and there she stood with my Uncle Tony. There was no need to pack shit; I had never unpacked. You couldn't tell me that I was staying there. Nine and a half hours later and I was home. The thirty two day stay with Kat was finally over.

After I came back to Aunt Debbie's from Michigan with Kat, I instantly felt like an outsider, as if I just didn't belong anymore. Something had changed. Uncle Tony always seemed irritated and easily annoyed with me or maybe it was the paranoia of the FBI kicking in our doors that had him always on edge.

Even Nikki and I went from best friends-sisters, to competitors. If Nikki would bring home all A's, I would be reminded of it every day, for weeks on end. My B's all of a sudden weren't good enough. Aunt Debbie's focus had switched to me full force. She was up my ass every move I made, even though Nikki was doing the same things I was doing. I was chasing boys but Nikki was chasing grown ass men. The older they were, the more she liked them.

I had begun to "act out" in school; that's what my Aunt would call it. I called it finding myself and learning my own identity, apart from being Nikki's shadow. I went to my own school, had my own friends, and wanted to be my own person. Still in all, my Aunt continued to remind me to "stop trying to be Nikki, stop mimicking her, be yourself." The more I took heed of her advice the more trouble I seemed to get into and the more my relationship with my Aunt grew colder. I started to be the leader in school rather than the follower. I stood out most of the time because of my inability to just "go with the flow". I always had questions as to *why* things were the way they were and "because" was not acceptable. This caused my teachers to think I was being disrespectful or trying to be a clown, which I was not, at least not all of the time. Although my behavior grades read all threes, my academic grades were A's and B's. Even with the change in my attitude at home and in school, I managed to graduate the eighth grade with second honors.

A month after I came back from Michigan with Kat, my Aunt Debbie, Uncle Tony and Nikki moved to the far northeast. I chose to stay at the house with Leigh since things had begun to get so ugly between Nikki and me. My Aunt Debbie had set me down one day and explained that things were going to have to be different now. She gave me a twenty five minute rundown on how nobody was supposed to know where her and my Uncle lived, their phone numbers and that if I was ever questioned by the police as to who Oscar Benson was, I was to say I didn't know. Oscar Benson was the identity that my Uncle had taken on a little while after I moved in with them. Even though nobody ever spoke directly to me about the things that were going on in our house, you had to be completely blind, or plain retarded not to know that my Uncle was hiding and running from the FBI. In a sense, we all were. I believe that's why I was sent to stay with Kat in Michigan. There wasn't a bone in me that thought Kat really wanted me to come move with her, just because. And when I called my Aunt Debbie that day that I had my first suicidal thoughts, I could tell by the way she said "taking care of something's" that things were happening with my Uncle that she didn't want me to see or know about. But I saw it all. I heard it all. I knew it all. I stayed quiet and pretended to be invisible like they treated me many of times when our house was *hot*. They provided a nice façade for our friends and neighbors and I enjoyed living it because dealing with the reality of my life was too much for little ole' me to digest.

CHAPTER 4

My first month of high school was full of culture shock. There were hundreds of kids moving about throughout the hallways. Everyone walked freely without any teachers escorting them or monitoring if they got from one class to the next, as they did in middle school. The kids didn't seem much like kids to me either. Some of the females wore tons of makeup, making them appear much older. Their jeans were super tight as were their t-shirts, exposing the print of their full C and even D cup sizes. The guys were tall, muscular and a many of them had facial hair. This was definitely a different crowd than what I was use to in middle school.

But I made the most of it. I went to class and always picked a seat in the middle of the class. I had quickly found that all the geeks, nerds, and dorks sat in the front of the class, kissing ass all day. And then, all the kids who couldn't read, add or subtract, or suffered from low-self-esteem or some other insecurity, sat in the back of the class hoping that the teacher wouldn't notice them.

Because I was quiet, I sometimes drew the attention of the obnoxious crowd that sat behind me. The guys would sit behind me and whisper all kinds of shit to me. The females just sucked their teeth and rolled their eyes. I never turned around or acknowledged them.

It bothered the guys, that unlike a lot of the other girls in the class, I kept to myself, pretended to not hear their shallow conversations, did my work but I clearly didn't fit in with the dorks, nerds, or geeks. Although my jeans weren't super tight, they hugged my legs nicely, displaying designer labels as my shirts laid perfectly against barely C cups. I wore my hair in a ponytail most days, unless I stayed late at the shop with Leigh for her to press my hair out for me. Most nights she didn't but when she did, she bitched, moaned and complain the entire time it took for her to press my hair. Two hours to be exact. I never got tired of the compliments that everyone always gave me about my "good" hair, I was thankful that Kat had at very least blessed me with that. And even though I got many compliments about my looks, I wasn't quite convinced. I was confused about what people actually saw when they looked at me. A lot of people would often call me Kitty. Mostly my great Aunts and older family friends who had watched Kat grow up. I hated that. They were insinuating that I was a baby her but I was nothing like her. And I didn't want to constantly be reminded that I was in the least bit tied to her. I didn't want people to see her when they saw me. When they would smile all in my face and call me Kitty, I would proudly correct them and say "Azhar!"

Besides Mr. George sick face would dance through my head every time someone said the name Kitty.

Nearing the end of my first month of school, I began to let the wrinkles in my forehead relax a little. Some of the girls in my class even began speaking to me. The first one was Camille. She had been sitting next to me for two weeks but I had never made eye contact with her. She was average, wore thick braids, like the ones Janet Jackson wore in the movie *Poetic Justice*, no name jeans, and plaid shirts. She never tried to match her outfits or accessorize even a little bit. She wore plain hooped earrings the size of a quarter and tucked her hideous looking shirts in her pants. But she was pretty. Her skin was flawless, no pimples or blemishes. Her eyes were dark brown and mysterious looking.

Camille and I had every class together. She knew a lot of people because she lived within walking distance of the school, unlike me; I lived almost out of the boundaries of the school zone so I knew hardly anyone. Camille and I exchanged numbers and became pretty close.

During gym class, Camille and I would sit on the sidelines; I'd people-watch and she'd write poetry in her journal. She was in love. She said that I would know I was in love when my every thought was consumed by someone and nothing else in the world mattered. She said the only way she could deal with being in love was by writing it down because her feelings were so deep. I asked her why she just didn't tell her boyfriend how she felt instead of writing them down all the time. Camille told me that boys were different than girls and that they didn't know how to properly express their emotions, that they weren't in touch with their emotional side like girls were. She said that boys "showed" their emotions with sex and girls expressed it through words and that was the reason girls talked more than boys. I shrugged my shoulders.

I wasn't in love, but I did have a sort-of boyfriend, Tyron. I had met him the summer that I graduated from middle school at a party. Tyron was my first introduction to boys. I had been checking for boys since I was about eleven or so but it wasn't until I saw Tyron that I knew that it all began and ended with a light-skinned, bow-legged guy. He was the epitome of gorgeous. His smile was so enticing. He stood about 5'7" and obviously was aware of his good looks because his demeanor was that of one confident motherfucker. I loved it, welcomed it even. But it was clear that Tyron and I were not a real thing.

He played ball and attended all the basketball games and tournaments that I wasn't allowed to attend yet. He worked and went to school and had very little spare time. Tyron also lived in the heart of North Philly, so he wasn't that easily accessible to me living across town in Uptown. Our summertime fling had gone cold once school started up, so here I was watching the guys run up and down the court during gym.

One Friday afternoon in gym, he was staring at me. And I was staring back. His name was Raheim.

He was kneeling down tying his Jordan's and boldly smiling, and I was stuck, unable to form a proper thought. I willed myself to look away but I couldn't. Then the bell rang and I stood up and thoughtlessly walked toward him. As I was nearing him, I caught the attention of the other guys standing around him, they all watched with big smiles upon their faces, giving me the approval that I really didn't need from them. I knew I looked good. My hair was neatly pressed with a part down the middle. My sweat pants had fit loosely around my waist, falling just right around my hips and exposing my flat stomach just a bit.

My tattoo was barely exposed, just the way I liked it. The red lips that I had gotten my eighth grade year had sent my ego through the roof. I was the only person in my school to have a tattoo. My teachers were all appalled after I showed it off the last week of school with my first pair of low-rider jeans. I was sent home that day too for being dressed inappropriately. Leigh had taken Nikki and I to get tattoos as school was nearing an end. I was surprised that my Aunt Debbie had allowed her. It hurt like hell. I thought I had died and went to hell during the thirty minute process. The man who did it tried to convince me to get my name or something on my arm like a lot of people were getting at that time but I didn't want my name. I knew my name, why did I need to have it permanently written on me? Besides, Leigh had got these fly eyes on her lower back and a fly tattoo of Mike's name on her so I wanted something equally as fly. Leigh was proud of my tattoo choice. She said it was classy and that I chose a good spot because I could let it be seen to those who I wanted to see it, or cover it up as if it was never there. And I did. My tattoo was low enough that I could wear jeans and a belly shirt and it not show or I could wear low-rider jeans and a belly shirt and it would peak out at you causing you to want to examine it more.

I walked right up to him, leaving barely enough space between us. The snickers from his friends added to my boldness. "Azhar." I let my name roll of my tongue with emphasis in the *Zhar* part to be sure he would remember how to pronounce it. He blushed and stuttered a little to get his name out. "Raheim"

I pulled a sharpie out of my binder, took his hand, and wrote down my name and number. "Call me, Rahiem". I smiled brightly, keeping eye contact. I walked confidently through his circle of friends not even excusing myself for bumping them. Camille called after me, and I stopped midway down the hall to wait for her and allow my heartbeat to slow down. I could hear it beating. It wasn't until I had walked away from Rahiem and his friends that I began to feel nervous.

"Do you know who that is?" Camille exclaimed in a hushed tone. I watched her excitement. Camille was usually very laid back. The only thing that really excited her was her boyfriend and those poems that she wrote. I pierced my lips together and leaned against my locker with one hand on my hip. "Rahiem." Her eyes lit up.

"Yes, that's Rahiem, Qua's brother. They are in that gang!"

"Gang? There aren't any gangs here in Philly. This ain't Compton." I couldn't help but laugh at Camille. She looked so serious.

"I mean, not like a killing gang but it's a corporation or something. They call themselves Real Players Corporation. It's like the best looking guys in the entire school. They all dress fly every day, only fuck with the most popular girls, and they all stick together. They move in a unit, all the time. Most of them have girlfriends that are seniors. Real fly chicks."

I smiled at Camille as I began to walk to class. "Like me."

Camille's facial expression revealed that a light bulb had gone off in her head. "Zhar, these guys are experienced. They aren't like you and me. They just want to fuck you and then their real girl friends will want to fight you."

I slowed my walking and turned towards Camille. "Well, I guess I'm going to have to be his real girlfriend then, 'cause you said guys express their selves through sex, right?"

That weekend Rahiem called me. Butterflies invaded my entire stomach when I heard his voice come through the phone. I closed my eyes and tried to calm myself. I put a mental check by his name in my head. I had a thing for winning and I set goals for myself daily. The moment Rahiem's eyes locked with mine, I knew I wanted him. I didn't know just how bad until Camille filled me in on his reputation. His reputation was just the icing on the cake. Rahiem was my type all the way. He was light-skinned with reddish, sandy brown hair and light freckles. He was bow-legged and about as tall as Tyron, thin build. I imagined that his nickname was Reds like most guys who shared his features.

We spoke on the phone for hours. I learned that he didn't go by any nickname, just Rahiem. He was the oldest of his five siblings and lived in Upton not far from our school. He was a real sports fan and played basketball or football almost every day. He was sixteen and in the eleventh grade. When he said eleventh grade I felt a little uneasy. My mind did what it did all the time, ran full speed into a million "what if" thoughts.

I closed my eyes again and told myself to stop it and relax. Rahiem was so chill. The tone in his voice was permanently at a level four while mine, which I had never paid attention to until then, was at a nine. Rahiem revealed to me that he didn't have a girlfriend, and that a girl that he had been seeing recently had slept with his brother. His voice didn't drop nor go up a level. I decided to use this as my opportunity to inquire about this gang that he was in.

"So you're a Real Player, huh?" I tried to mask my smile as if he could somehow see me grinning from ear to ear.

His chuckle was cute. "Oh man." He laughed a little more. "Where'd you get that from?"

"Around." It was at this point that I had realized that I had colored the entire front and back of my note book and that my ink pen was now inkless. I glanced at the clock on my dresser and three hours had passed since the start of our conversation. Leigh was not home yet and probably wouldn't be home for a few more hours.

"Around where?"

"Around school, duh. You're in a Corporation, right, and it's called Real Players?" Rahiem continued to chuckle as if he was amused. After about three minutes of an awkward silence, I decided to move on from that question. "So no girlfriend. I don't believe that." I shook my head. I really couldn't believe that. Who in their right fucking mind wouldn't want to be his girlfriend?

"What you went to private school or somethin'?" His question pulled me out of my own head.

"What? No. Why you say that?"

"Because the way you talk."

"How exactly is it that I talk?"

"Like that. Proper. White."

I was confused. What did he mean "white?" Could Raheim tell I had taken a professional communication class through my mentally gifted program? That I studied etiquette and public speaking? Either way, I was offended. Was he saying I sounded snobbish?

"What does it sound like to sound white?" I demanded to know.

Rahiem laughed again, and I picked up on it being something he did whenever he was nervous. "You just don't sound like a black girl that's all. And when you curse it sounds weird, like a white person."

I had never heard this before. I was silent. I tried to play my voice back in my own head to see if it sounded "white". I dismissed Rahiem's comments. I felt flustered and nervous. What if my voice was bothering him? Was it annoying? I changed the subject quickly instead of allowing dead air to suffocate us. "Tell me about your parents."

"What you want to know? My mom works at a nursing home and my dad does, like, construction."

"Why did they divorce?"

"They never married."

"Oh. Why not?" The words escaped my lips before I had a chance to rethink it.

"I don't know. You got a lot of questions but you ain't saying nothing bout you."

"What is there to say? What you see is what you get?"

"Nah, that's not true. I can tell there's more to you. Tell me bout you."

I thought of many different things to say to Rahiem just then and as the images flashed around in my head my chest begin to feel heavy. Images of Kat shooting up, the smell of burned glass, the leather belts smacking against my wet skin, Desmond, Kat's burned fingertips, crack pipes, the back of Cash's head as she walked out the door and out of my life forever.

"Azhar" Rahiem broke into my thoughts. "I have to call you back my brother needs to use the phone."

By December Rahiem and I had been kickin' it heavy. We talked almost every day on the phone and Leigh had taken a liking to him. She had even begun allowing him to come over on the weekends while I baby-sat her children.

One Saturday afternoon as I let Rahiem in, he had a strange look on his face, instead of the usual smile or grin that I had become accustomed to. "What's wrong?"

A few seconds elapsed before Rahiem answered. He seemed to be in deep thought. "Yo, I think somebody outside watching ya house?"

An uneasy feeling came over me. I didn't respond. Instead I walked in the kitchen to buy myself some time to think of a response. I hoped enough time would lapse and I could move the conversation into another direction without having to even entertain that statement. "You want something to drink?" I called to him from the kitchen?

"Nawl, I'm good."

While in the kitchen I dipped into the pantry and closed the door behind me. I dialed Nikki's pager number and put 1610 behind it. She was on her way to stay the weekend with me and my Uncle was bringing her. I needed to warn them. It had been a few months since I had seen anyone sitting on the corner in their black Camry or black Navigators. They were not good at hiding. In fact, I think they wanted us to know they were there. We lived in an all-black neighborhood and my family drove the flyest cars on the block but here they were, pale white men, wearing shades in the winter, sitting in better cars than anyone around with tinted windows.

Nikki called me back immediately, 1610 was our code that they were outside. We all had pagers and always used codes when paging each other. If you didn't put a code behind the number then that was probably because you weren't family and we weren't going to call you back, no matter what phone number you used or how many times you paged us. We never used 911. It was a dead giveaway and while many of times it was important if we were paging, we wanted to make sure we specified just how important or what the page pertained to. 911 drove everyone into panic and my Uncle taught us never to panic when dealing with this situation or that we would make careless mistakes like, mentioning names or giving out phone numbers over the phone, which was a big no no. Our phones were tapped sometimes and when they were, it was plainly obvious. That's when we all got pagers. But we never kept the same one for too long.

I let the phone ring four times before I picked it to let Nikki know that they weren't in the house. "Hello," I answered casually. I assumed Rahiem was probably listening too.

"Hey. So, I'm not going to stop and get a cheesesteak after all." That was Nikki confirming that they were out there and she wasn't coming.

"Okay, I'm gone call you back, I have company."

That afternoon I was extremely nervous to be around Rahiem. My mind raced with thoughts of the feds busting in my house. My heart beat so furiously I just knew Rahiem could hear it. I turned on the TV to fill the empty space of silence. He looked uncomfortable sitting there on the long couch as I sat in the love seat across from him. I could tell he didn't know what to say, but neither did I.

As I sat and thought, I hated my entire life. Those thoughts had never crossed my mind until then. I had always hated situations, but it was everything about living that I hated now. My Aunt Bobbie was vicious and didn't know the meaning of love. My sister Cash was illiterate and homeless, and no one kept in contact with her now that she had aged out of the system. I had a little brother that I didn't know and who probably had HIV thanks to Kat. My picture perfect life at the Jones's was a fraud. It was faker than a three dollar bill.

Prada sneakers and Tiffany's bracelets paired with other expensive designer brands kept people talking about the obvious, I looked good. My newly developed "I don't give a fuck" attitude helped me cope with things beyond my control like gossip and envy. Shopping with Leigh on a daily for new, better, even flyer, more expensive designer items clouded my sense of reality.

But Rahiem, Rahiem seemed to pull me out the clouds, force me to think about shit that I never wanted to think about again in life. He adored his mother and had authentic friendships with everyone in his Corporation, though he never admitted nor denied being a part of one, I knew he was. He seemed to be doing something so simple. Living. Me, I wasn't living. I merely existed, and inside I was dead. I don't think I ever was alive inside. I don't think I ever knew happiness, joy or even love.

Hearing him speak about his brother, I could tell they had a crazy tight bond. Nikki and Leigh, though I genuinely loved and adored them like my own blood sisters, I began to see sides of them that couldn't possibly be love. I hadn't ever experienced jealousy from a family member, so it hurt me deeply when Nikki began treating me like a stranger rather than the sister that she professed to everyone that I was. Nikki and Leigh had their own differences which spawned rapidly into an all-out war. I don't know how or why it began but it was mind blowing at times to watch the hateful things they would do and say to one another. It became evident that I wasn't playing with the same deck of cards as them when I found myself to be the official "outsider". It was at this point that I was faced with the reality that I could write Jones at the end of my name all I wanted, I could introduce my friends to my Aunt Debbie as my mom until my eyes turned blue. I could tuck Cash, Desmond and Kat so far back in my mind until they didn't exist to me all I wanted. The fact still remained, they were my mother, father and sister; not Debbie, Tony, Leigh and Nikki. When I was forced to think about it like that, tears broke through my wall of steel bars that I had placed long ago in front of my eyes forbidding tears to seep through.

My Aunt Debbie had helped me create this wall. I was always an emotional person. It seemed that everything in me was soft and vulnerable and at any given moment, my emotions would invade my eyes and spill out in the form of tears. For two summers before I moved in with my Aunt Debbie, I would visit her and Nikki. Every time I began to cry she would gently, yet sternly command me to stop crying. When I sniffed my last sniff and wiped my last tear she would say "now, use your words. Express yourself. Tell me how you're feeling. Don't cry cause I can't understand that and that's for babies and weak adults."

Whenever I fell and hurt myself, she would be standing right there with her hand on her petite hips waiting for me to wipe my tears before speaking to her. My Aunt Debbie was gentle, yet emotionless.

"Azhar, why are you crying?"

"I'm not." I tried to crack a smile to trick my brain into thinking I was happy so that the tears would stop falling mid-way. I stood to my feet quickly and teardrops landed on my hands. Rahiem stood and walked toward me with his arms out.

"Stop, please, please don't touch me." It was a demand rather than a request. I was feeling hypersensitive at the moment and I was so angry with myself that I had allowed Rahiem to see it. I needed him to leave. I needed him out of my space. It was all good as long as he wasn't in my real world. But there he was, in my house, witnessing my real life and my real feelings which not even I was capable of dealing with.

"You have to go. I can't explain right now. I, I'mma call you later. You have to go." I walked quickly to the front door never making eye contact with Rahiem. I wiped my eyes dry as I moved. When I got the front door I realized that Rahiem wasn't right behind me as I expected to him to be. Didn't he hear what I had said? What part didn't he understand? Rahiem stood in the same place where I had left him.

"Are you putting me out after I just caught the bus all the way over here in this freezing weather?"

I was annoyed that Rahiem was questioning me, but I was more annoyed that I still felt like I needed to cry, and it was taking everything out of me not to breakdown right then and there. I felt a full blown crying spell coming on. The lump in my throat was mounting. My heart began to pick up speed as the thump became louder. I ran passed Rahiem up the stairs into the bathroom, slamming the door behind me. I turned on the water in the shower, tub and sink, hoping to create enough noise to muffle my screams.

Over the past year I had developed a coping mechanism. Instead of crying, I would scream. I would scream loudly. Sometimes, if I was home alone, I would scream until I couldn't scream anymore, until my throat was completely raw and I was horse. But right now, at this moment, as much as I either needed to cry or scream, I was scared to do either in fear the Rahiem would hear me and think I was completely retarded or even worse-weak and crazy. Rage. That's what I felt. Rage consumed me and I needed to release it. My eyes darted around the bathroom searching for something, but what? I did not know.

Our bathroom was surrounded by floor to ceiling mirrors on two of the four walls and for a second I contemplated smashing them but that would be too much to explain and way too much to clean up. Scented candles lined the Jacuzzi tub. Without even thinking I threw four of them to the floor shattering them into hundreds of pieces. But I still felt anger, rage and panic. I ran to the door and opened it before Rahiem had a chance to climb the steps.

"I'm okay, I just dropped the candle. I'll be down in a second." I said calmly as I fought back tears.

As I went to try and sweep the glass into a pile with my hands a tiny piece pricked my finger causing blood to gush to the surface. A pleasant surprise came over me. It was a small glimpse of relief. The prick from the glass was painful, yes, but in a very strange kind of way, it felt good. I picked up a larger piece of the glass and sat down on the side of the tub. I held the glass to my wrist. I thought about Kat. She had attempted suicide on many occasions, I was told. The thought of that made me quiver. I erased that thought just as quickly as it appeared. I wasn't Kat and damn sure wasn't weak like her.

Those were my thoughts but the vision in my head played out a scene of a young girl with long jet black hair, longer than mine. She sat on the floor with something in her hand as blood rushed from her wrist onto the tan carpet. I couldn't see her face. Her hair covered it as she was huddled over. I could hear her sobs clearly. Just as I was trying to erase the scene from my head, the girl lifted her head. Her eyes were piercing, dark, and hurt shined through like a beautiful summer day. It was Kat.

I opened my left hand and held the glass with my right. I dug deeply into the center of my hand with the glass carving the letter A for my name. The first cut was worst of all. It reminded me of when I got my tattoo. It felt like someone was burning me with fire. But it quickly faded. The next two cuts to complete the A brought all relief. My heartbeat slowed, the lump in my throat dissipated, and my brain even seemed to slow down enough for me to think clearly. I heard voices. Oh shit, Rahiem! I jumped up and grabbed a hand towel from the back of the door before opening it.

"Rahiem, are you okay? I'm just cleaning this glass up."

"Yeah, I'm good just watching TV."

CHAPTER 5

"Do you know what HIV is?" I softly asked Rahiem.

"Yeah, why?"

"What is it, exactly?"

"It's a disease." He stated casually as if it weren't known to be one of the nastiest disease yet.

"I know it's a disease, but like, how do you get it? Where does it come from?"

"Why are you asking me these questions?"

"Because I wanna know?" I spat, frustrated.

"I don't know where it comes from. You can get it by having unprotected sex. I guess. It's called the monkey causes once you get it, it's on you like a monkey clinging to your back"

I thought about all the unprotected sex that Kat probably had. It made me think about Kat fucking some strange man or dozens of men to get high. What were drugs? I wondered. What was so good about it that people loved it more than their own flesh and blood; more than their own kids? Suddenly, a picture of a little girl with two long ponytails hanging one down each side of her head appeared in my head. She was crying and begging a woman not to leave. Her body was clasped tightly around the woman's leg. The little girl was me and the woman was Kat. I saw hurt and pain in her eyes, so why was she leaving? I imagined that she was going off to get high again. *Why didn't she love me more than the drugs?* I wondered.

"Azhar, you hear me?"

"Yeah, I hear you." I answered Rahiem but really, I didn't hear anything he had said.

"No you didn't."

"My bad, what'd you say?"

"I said, why you asking me about HIV?"

I thought hard before answering Rahiem but for some reason I didn't want to lie anymore. We had been dating for six months and I wanted to tell him or somebody the truth about me. I wanted to release all of my thoughts, all of my frustrations and anger. I wanted somebody to hear me, to understand me and most of all, to help me understand me.

"My mom is HIV positive. Does that mean she's going to die?" I could feel the tears building up. I fought hard to keep them from falling. I wouldn't cry though. Crying was for weak people like Kat. She was weak. She wasn't strong like me; she couldn't fight her addictions.

Years had passed since I had found out that Kat had HIV, but still no one told me what it was or what it would do to Kat. I had heard stories about people deteriorating and dying, or having lesions on their skin, but Kat didn't have any lesion and she wasn't deteriorating, so I didn't know what to think. Rahiem remained silent for just as long as me.

"Is she?" I asked again.

"I don't know. I don't think she can die from HIV. She's just sick, right?"

"I don't know. I don't know much about her." I confessed.

"She doesn't look sick."

He was right, she didn't look sick, but then it occurred to me—Rahiem thought Aunt Debbie was my mom. I needed to tell him about Kat, but then I would have to tell him everything, and it was all so confusing to me I knew he would be lost too. Nothing made any sense to me.

"Azhar, you want me to call you tomorrow?" Rahiem quizzed.

"No, I was just thinking. Rahiem, I have to tell you something but you have to promise me that you won't tell anyone. I mean no one!" I didn't know what I would do if people found out about the real me. What would people think if they knew my mother abandoned me when I was just a baby? How would they act if they knew she had HIV? And what about her addiction and her turning tricks? My life would fall apart if people knew the real Azhar Washington. Then again, who was Azhar Washington? I had been who people wanted and expected me to be for so long, I didn't even know who I was.

"What is it? You can tell me anything." Rahiem sounded so reassuring but I could

imagine the thoughts that would run through his head when he heard all of the craziness I was about to try and explain to him.

"This is so hard and I… I don't know how to say this. I don't know where to begin. " My voice faded out as my mind went into deep thought again. Just as I was about to remember something, Rahiem interrupted my train of thought.

"Zhar, would you just tell me, I mean it's not the end of the world. Whatever it is, it will be ok." Rahiem sounded so convincing. If only it was that easy.

"Debbie isn't my mom and Leigh and Nikki aren't my sisters." I blurted out.

Rahiem remained silent for a while before saying, "You act like you were about to tell me that you were raped as a child or something?"

"Well you're close," I explained. "I was raped of my childhood. My mom's name is Kat. She's HIV positive. I haven't seen her in almost a year."

"Well where is she?" Rahiem asked.

"I don't know," I shrugged my shoulders as if Rahiem could see me over the phone. "I've never known where she was. She has to live somewhere, though; she could have taken me with her!" I cried unconsciously. "I'm not weak!" I shouted. "I'm just angry!"

"You don't have to be weak to cry, Azhar." Rahiem said softly. "You're hurt, that's all."

"I'm not hurt!" I yelled, sitting straight up in my bed. "Nothing she can do to me can hurt me. I have been through hell and back all by myself. There's nothing that anyone can ever do to hurt me. I've had the worst beatings that you can ever imagine. I've gotten beatings in the tub while all soapy and beatings in the sink while getting my hair washed. I've gotten beatings with the belt buckles and branch off trees. I've even gotten beatings with rulers, brushes, wire hangers and extension cords. So don't tell me that I'm hurt, I know when I'm hurt, and Kat cannot hurt me. She has never hurt me."

"Azhar, calm down!" Rahiem hissed. It was as if he wanted to yell at me but was in the company of others. I had never heard Rahiem raise his voice. It wasn't in his demeanor. He was so calm, so soft, yet rugged. I flopped down on my bed. I had found myself walking in circles.

"You're saying so much, I don't know what you're talking about. I get that your mom is somewhere, and that she left you and that she is HIV positive but like I said… it's not the end of the world."

I hated when people could so easily minimize my situation, and Rahiem had done it twice in less than five minutes. Who did he think he was?

That night, I told Rahiem everything about me, about the real Azhar Faith Washington, at least all that I knew myself. I told Rahiem the story of how my mom sold me for drugs when I was two years old. She sold me to a white couple who couldn't have kids for five hundred dollars. The family didn't want to give me back and Desmond's family had to threaten to call the cops. Rahiem was speechless; exactly what I thought he would be. I had gotten so lost in my own thoughts that I didn't know if he was listening or not.

"Azhar you don't have to tell me anymore if you don't want to." He said finally. But I wanted to. I wanted and needed to tell someone everything that I had held in for years. Rahiem was the first person that I had ever told anything about me, or Kat, or even Desmond. I told him how my father killed my Uncle and how he went crazy. I told him how, when I was two and lived with Kat, she left me with Desmond and his new girlfriend for two days and I caught lice in my eyebrows and had to have them shaved off and my hair cut off.

"And when I was ten, I found out that my mom was HIV positive. I didn't know what that was then. I'm still a little confused. Last year my mom came back and told me that she had contracted HIV by being raped. She said that she wasn't sure if that's where it came from but, not long before she found out that she was positive, she had been gang raped," one tear rolled down my cheek into my mouth as I began to say, "But my mom has been doing drugs and turning tricks since before I was born. The doctor told her that she could have been HIV positive for ten years now and not shown one sign. That rules me out, but, but you never really know. She never had been tested before then. When I was born, she had a blood transfusion. She could have gotten it through that. No one is sure."

"So you're saying that you can be HIV positive too?" I didn't expect Rahiem to be so forward about this, but really what did I expect? I came back just as forward and straight up as he was. "I don't know, I'm saying. I don't know what I'm saying. I'm just telling you all that I know."

"Have you ever been tested?"

"No, I'm a virgin. I guess I never thought about it, even after Kat told me. The doctor said that, more than likely, I have nothing to worry about."

"You're a virgin?" Rahiem repeated. I could hear the smile in Rahiem's voice. "You sound so experienced."

"No, you just assume that I should be experienced. Why?" I questioned.

"I don't know, the way you act, the way you carry yourself." Admitted Rahiem.

"How do I act? I don't act any different than any other girl I know." Rahiem paused for a moment. "Yes you do," he laughed. "And you know you do." He said as a matter of fact. His indirect comments brought a smile to my face.

"No, I don't." I couldn't help but to blush.

"Azhar, you walk around like you the shit and can't anybody tell you shit."

"So, that doesn't mean I'm experienced in having sex."

Rahiem blew me off with a fake laugh. "Anybody with as much arrogance as you better be experienced in everything."

"I'm not arrogant. I'm just confident and people don't know how to handle that because of the lack of their own confidence." I retorted.

"Alright, if you say so."

"And I am experienced, in life!" after a pregnant pause I said, "I've been thinking about going and getting tested. I'm just so scared."

"You know Azhar, I really like you. I mean, I care about you, a lot. I care about you like, I love you." I thought that time had stopped for a moment before I realized that it had not. "And, I've never felt this way about anyone in my life. We have kissed a lot so if you've got it, then so do I. It's already too late."

My heart began to race and pound uncontrollably. Oh my God is all I thought. I had completely forgotten about that. I wanted to say something but no words came to my mind, instead tears came to my eyes.

"Azhar, don't worry, I just got a complete physical two three weeks ago, everything was fine. I've been getting tested for the last three years. Azhar, did you hear me? I love you." Rahiem whispered.

"Prove it." I demanded.

"Prove what?"

My emotions were running crazy, like how I felt sometimes when Kat pop back into my life. I was happy and sad all at once. I didn't know if I wanted to cry or jump for joy. My brain was officially fried for the night. The only one thing I wanted to make sure I did was put a mental double check by Rahiem's name. I had him. He loved me. And he said it first without me having to write love letters or poetry or do back flips or even fuck him. But now, if he said he loved me, I wanted him to prove it like Camille said. People who loved each other made love, right?

"Rahiem, I hope you mean what you are saying, or you will be sorry."

The next morning Leigh was not home. As always, she hadn't come home from work and had gone straight to Atlantic City instead. I was flustered. Her children were up and hungry for food which we had none of and I was about to be late for school which would make me miss the hangout. I threw some pancakes together in about nine minutes flat and ran to take a shower. After my three minute shower I stood facing my closet as I pondered what to wear. Jeans of course but which ones? About thirty pairs of jeans of every rinse were neatly stacked to the ceiling of my closet.

A pair of super stretch Jordache jeans peaked out at me with the tags still hanging on them. These weren't the newest of my collection but they were the most expensive that Leigh had recently got me from her trip to Bermuda. I grab them and popped the tags and emptied three dresser draws on my bed to find the perfect shirt. It looked dark and gloomy out so I grabbed a white baby tee that had the letters FCUK written in black across the chest. I slipped on a pair of Jordan's; the thirteen's that I had recently seen Rahiem and his crew rockin a few days before their actual release date. I had begged and begged Leigh for these and finally she got them, two weeks later than I had hoped for but there they were, lookin fresh on my size five foot.

Just as I was about to pick up the phone and try to locate Leigh I heard the front door close. "Zahar, Mike is outside waiting to take you to school." I rolled my eyes at Leigh as she click clocked her five-inch Prada boots against the hardwood floor so carelessly. I loved Leigh, loved her like we came through the same pussy, but ever since she hooked up with Mike, she wasn't the same Ashleigh that I once admired so much and aspired to be. She wasn't ambitious or strong willed anymore. She no longer seemed to take pride in being a mother or go getter like she once preached to me about. At this point the only thing that Leigh cared about was being with Mike and at any cost. Mike was Leigh's first priority. Not her kids and not her money like she use to always proclaim. Leigh would often work late at her salon but now she would leave in the middle of the day to ride shotgun with Mike to Atlantic City. Their weekend trips to AC turned into week long trips to AC. A little fun and games quickly turned into a full blown addiction that Leigh seemed to be losing the battle to. It annoyed me. I was disappointed in Leigh. She was so much better than this. She was becoming everything she told me not to be. I assumed her love for Mike was greater than her love for money or her kids. As this thought passed through my head, I cringed a bit. This was a trait that Kat had. The ability to love something more than your kids was weak. Leigh was becoming like Kat, weak for Mike. I resented her for that. *I'll never be weak for a man*, I thought.

I sat in the passenger seat of the black on black Benz that Mike adored and called his baby. The beat from little Kim's "Big Momma Thing" blared through the speakers engulfing the entire car. I crossed my ankles and adjusted my puffy, Baby Phat powder blue coat.

"So what's going on little Leigh" Mike smiled brightly.

"Nothing much, about to be late for school." I checked the side view mirror, the feds were following us. I sucked my teeth.

"What's wrong?"

"Men in Black, story of my fifteen year old life. But I guess I can't complain huh?" I was always straight with Mike, no filter. Respectful but no sugar coating shit. I guess that's the least he could give me. He knew I could see through his bullshit so he never tried to act like he was high and mighty. He didn't ever preach to me or try to play the 'dad' role. He also knew that I knew what went on with him and Leigh late at night when the kids were sleep. The arguments, the fights, the abuse. Mike treaded lightly with me and I liked it that way. He always called me little Leigh because he said that Leigh and I favored one another more than Leigh and Nikki did. It was the skin complexion that made people think that, I assume. Nikki was light and Leigh and I, well I wouldn't necessarily say we were dark skin but we were browner than Nikki.

"Oh yeah, them." Mike leaned back harder in his chair. If you didn't know any better you would think Mike was a young bull. He drove with his seat nearly in the back seat, his hat pulled so low on his head that you could barely see his face and his music blasting so loud it could be heard a block away. Mike drove me to school every morning and every day older girls would come up to me asking if he was my boyfriend. When I said no, they would ask if I could hook them up.

"So, you into sneakers now, huh?" Mike laughed.

I suppressed my smile. "Yeah, they hot right? I flexed my foot and admired my footwork. Mike laughed at me flexin. "So, who is he?"

My smile invaded my entire face. "Common, you already know. I know Leigh already told you."

"Yeah, she said you got a little boyfriend. But I'm asking you about him. Do Debbie and Tony know about him? What's his name? How old is he? Yall," He paused and stopped at a red light and starred me dead in my eyes "Yall, you know. Are yall?" I began to feel a little hot all of a sudden. I smoothed my hand over my hair, up into my ponytail and checked the time on my pager. I was so uncomfortable. Who the hell did Mike think he was asking me question about my personal life? He wasn't my father! Shit, he wasn't even a dad to Leigh's kids.

"Alright little Leigh, don't be out here," he paused and smiled at me. "You know. Don't bring no babies home."

"Babies! Who the fuck want a baby?" My words escaped my lips before I could catch hold of them. They were out; there was nothing I could do now. I stared out the window. "Sorry. Sorry for cursing like that."

"It's cool." Mike said nonchalantly. "I see you growing up little Leigh. Just be careful. Don't let none of these nothing ass little boys fuck you over and hurt you." His words pierced my ears, froze me in place. Mike was always talking to me about real shit but he never talked like this, so raw and uncut. I guess he had no choice at this point. I had just made it clear that I wasn't all that innocent like everyone thought I was. We pulled in front of my school. I opened the door to get out.

"I don't like little boys Mike", I turned to look back at him, "and ain't nobody fucking me over or hurting me either." He smiled. I smiled. I shut the door and hurried to class.

Finally in class, I took the only seat available to the far left of the class in the front. I nodded at Camille and Naja, another girl that I had begun hanging with in school. Once seated, I slumped far down in my seat and relaxed my shoulders a bit. The class was rowdy and the teacher's words were barely audible. The tall, thin, frail white man had his back to the class and rambled on as if he had everyone's attention. Unless he had forgotten his hearing aid, I assumed this was his way of dealing with the class, by not dealing with us at all. I tried for the first seventeen minutes or so to listen to what he was saying but, all of the other side conversations, singing, beat making contest and gossip columns were too distracting. Besides, there was three girls standing outside the class pointing and staring at me, or maybe they were pointing and staring at the retarded jocks that sat behind me.

Third period was first lunch and I attended that religiously because it was one of the best lunch periods. My actual lunch period was fifth, I attended that as well. At third period lunch, I mingled with a few people from around my way that were close with Nikki. They were all juniors and seniors. I fit in perfectly though. Once the bell rang, I made my way to stairway four. I reached the top of the steps and Rahiem walked through the door. He smiled. His smile was so innocent, so shy like.

"So what's up?"

"Nuffin much. I'm 'bout to leave, I'm tired."

"Leave? Leave school?"

"Yeah."

"Oh," I closed my mouth which I was sure was hanging open. I had never ditched school, though Nikki often told me about how her and her friends would. I leaned my back against the wall and pondered my next sentence.

"You coming?"

I was at a loss for words. I wanted to say hell no! Where the hell would we go in the middle of the day when we were supposed to be at school? What if Leigh or Mike, or better yet what if my Aunt Debbie saw me outside of school during school hours? I'd surely be shipped back to Michigan with Kat. Lord knows if my Uncle Tony caught me, he'd probably beat me right there where I stood. If I said no, Rahiem would think I was immature. He would think I was being the fifteenth year old that I was. I could feel my hands beginning to sweat, my stomach begin to feel queasy. I took out a stick of mint gum because it always calmed me when I was in stressful situations.

"Yeah, I'll go."

We took the steps to the ground floor and left out of a side door. There was no security or anyone at the door to keep anyone from leaving, as we did. We walked about three blocks before I said anything. I kept looking around at passing cars.

"Where are we going Rahiem?"

"To my house. My mom is at work until 4:00pm."

I felt panicked. Who would be at Rahiem's house then? What if we got caught? Would his mom call Leigh? Would the school call home and tell Leigh that I skipped some of my classes? Twelve blocks of worrying and finally we walked up the steps to an apartment. Inside was small, and gloomy. It reminded me of Kat's apartment in Michigan.

When I sat down on the grey couch I had no idea that I would lose my virginity that day. It felt nothing like I had imagined. Nothing about it felt good. I was nervous and could feel my hands trembling. My heart didn't melt like people portrayed on TV. There wasn't one single romantic thing about it, earth shattering or mind blowing. In fact, midway through I told Rahiem to let me get on top like I had saw in pornos that came on late at night. This felt better, at least now I was in control. I moved slowly, watching Rahiem's reactions. With each sound that escaped his lips I grew more confident in what I was doing. I watched him watch me. I studied his breathing patterns, how he tensed up every time I clinched my muscle tighter. Before I knew it Rahiem had wrapped his arms around me tightly, holding me in place as louder moans escaped his lips. His eyes were shut tightly as he pressed his head deeply into my chest. After a moment, his grip loosened and his body went limp. I didn't know what was happening. He sat back and let out a nervous laugh. I stared at him watching for a clue as to what was going to happen next.

"Wow." He finally said.

Now I was embarrassed. "Wow, what?"

"That was great."

"Oh really?"

"Yes really." He said.

"Oh." I didn't know what else to say. I made my way to the bathroom and closed and locked the door behind me. I leaned my back against the door to allow the door to catch all my weight as I felt like I weighed a ton.

"Okay, Azhar." I whispered to myself. *"Now what?"* I slid down to the floor because I was beginning to get feeling back into my legs and they were begging me to sit down and rest them. The white and pink tiled floor was cold but soothing. My once neat ponytail was cocked to the side with the twist tie barely holding it in place. The powder blue nail polish on my toes caught my eyes as I examined my legs trying to figure out why they were still trembling. I pressed my legs firmly against the floor trying to control them. I couldn't. A heap of emotion rushed over me as I allowed myself to feel for the first time since I had entered the small apartment. My fingers were tingly and sweat was building up. I could feel perspiration under my arms and around the back of my neck. My legs were now clammy and stuck to the tile floor. I didn't like the feeling that was building in my chest. A ball of laughter erupted from deep within. I caught it the moment it echoed off the walls.

Bitch, you just fucked him. You fucked him good, I heard. I held my hands over my mouth tightly to suppress the powerful laughter that was trying desperately to escape. I was startled at my thoughts and tone of the voice in my head. It sounded like Kat.

You're beautiful! It was Kat's voice again or so I thought. I couldn't tell for sure. I stared at the mirror, examining the reflection. Then, I remembered. While I was riding Rahiem he repeatedly said that. He said I was beautiful. A smile spread across my face as I absorbed the words. "Yes, I am fucking beautiful!" I whispered barely audible. Smiling from ear to ear I felt more confident than ever about my looks. I washed myself off and redressed myself. My hair was a fucking mess, but I liked it. Still, I couldn't go home with my hair all wild like that so I grabbed a thick wooden brush, wet it, and brushed my hair neatly back into a ponytail securing it with my twist tie.

CHAPTER 6

My insides felt weird. I wasn't sure if I was coming down with a stomach virus or what. But I felt funny. I sat in the tub replaying what little of my first sexual experience I remembered. For some odd reason much of it was a blur. I wanted to call Nikki and spill all the details to her like I imagined sisters were supposed to do with things like this but I didn't. I couldn't. Over the past few months Nikki and I were hardly speaking and I wasn't even sure why.

"He loves me." The words blurted out my mouth like I had been holding them capture forever.

"What? Who?" asked Camille.

"Rahiem!"

"Azhar, you are crazy. He told you that?" Camille smile could be felt. I guess mine could also. Our voices were squeaky and high pitched as we screamed and laughed and I even hopped around holding my towel over my naked body. My lips just would not allow me to hold it in anymore. I had to tell someone.

"Yes! Yes, he told me a few weeks ago and she *showed* me." I felt like a little kid on Christmas morning, though none of my Christmases were ever that exciting but TV had a way of showing you exactly how the rest of the world was living.

"Showed you?! Showed you *how?*"

I paused. Camille's words didn't sound too enthusiastic. "He showed me like how you said boys show girls they love them." My words slowly traveled out of my mouth. I didn't feel too excited anymore. Camille had sucked all my excitement out of me just that fast.

"You mean you had sex with him? Oh Azhar."

"Oh Azhar? What do you mean oh Azhar! Rahiem loves me. He told me a few weeks ago, *before* we had sex. I know what you are thinking but it's not like that. Rahiem isn't like those loser ass boys, fucking every chick with a pussy." Camille was silent and it annoyed me. "So you mean to tell me that Sean can love you but Rahiem can't love me?"

"Azhar that's not what I'm saying. I'm just saying that Rahiem is-, he is so different than Sean- "

"Yup, you are correct Camille. Rahiem and Sean are different in the way that Sean is a hood nigga and Rahiem is not! He's a decent guy with a decent family. His mother raised him!" My chest was rising and falling heavily with each word.

"His mother raised him? What does that mean? Everybody's mother raises them. That doesn't mean anything and Sean is not a hood nigga!"

"Camille," I sat on the edge of my bed and unconsciously crossed my legs, something that my Aunt Debbie had taught me when I was six. *Sit like a lady, cross your legs, don't slouch, shoulders back, chin up*; she would say. Now, I did it out of habit. I breathed heavily. "Sean is a hood nigga," I said matter of fact. "I see him in the mornings standing outside on the side of the building lighting up. That dark skin on his lips isn't natural either. He attends zero classes per day, has no ambition, drive or desire to be anything."

Silence filled the phone line.

"Bye Azhar."

Dear Diary,

I haven't written to you in so long. I have so much to say but where do I begin? Camille and I made up; she apologized to me after not speaking to me for three days. I'm glad she did because I missed talking to her and I couldn't wait to share my poems with her. Rahiem is...I don't know. He's everything. Every time I see him, my heart smiles. Is that possible? It feels like it. My entire body does a dance, the excitement builds and builds and builds. I feel like I'm high above earth, floating. It's a feeling I use to get when I was about four or five years old and Desmond would come and get me for the day. He would come to Aunt Bobbie's house on a Saturday afternoon, always in the summer and we would spend the entire day traveling to different family member's houses. Everyone always seemed so happy to see me. The love felt so good. Those days seemed long but never long enough. The moment we would turn the corner to Aunt Bobbie's house, my heart would fall into the pit of my stomach. The life in me would be snatched away-just like that. Desmond would bounce me down off his shoulders where I held on for dear life as we traveled through the streets. He would reach down, holding my little self in his huge arms. Even though he always reeked of some cheap six pack of beer and the menthol scent from the cigarettes was almost unbearable, I stomached it with a smile and looked forward to his kiss on my cheek.

With tears in my eyes, I looked Desmond square in the face "Dad!" But before I could get any other words out Desmond would say, "Baby Girl, I'm gone come get you next weekend, so you make sure you be ready, alright?" The first few times Desmond said this to me, my heart swelled with joy and excitement and I just couldn't wait for the weekend to roll around again but you know how Desmond is. Lies. Remember what he said to me? "Baby Girl, promises are made to be broken." He would say with such certainty. When I get older, if I ever have kids-which I doubt but if God blesses me with children, I'm never breaking a promise to them. My word is going to be like gold. Bet on that!

But yeah, Rahiem makes me feel all, breathless. And the sex, well, I don't know. I'm still waiting to touch heaven or something magnificent like people say is supposed to happen. But he seems to enjoy it so much. So much that he moans my name. Now that, that sends chills up my spine. To see him cumin-I think that's what Nikki called it. Yes, I broke down and told Nikki about Rahiem and I. Watching Rahiem in that state is the highlight of sex for me. It makes me feel powerful. To make such a strong and arrogant guy like Rahiem, lose control, unnhunn-yup. I got him.

The halls were empty. Quiet even. I stood in front of my locker. The word *bitch* was written on the front of my locker in black magic marker. I rolled my eyes. *People will be jealous of you all your life, Azhar. You won't understand it until you are much older, when you realize who you really are. You are different.* Kat's voice swirled around in my head. I was in elementary school when I began getting teased for having long hair and being knock-kneed. The boys would call me Pippy Long Stocking and pull my pony-tales that hung to the middle of my back. The girls weren't all that nice either-they mocked my voice because of the way I talked, which in my eyes wasn't any different than the way they spoke.

I thought about which bitch could have wrote on my locker. A lot of faces appeared in my head. I wasn't all that friendly with anyone in school. I really didn't fit into a particular group. The first couple of weeks were awkward but it was when I began seeing Rahiem that I begin to feel the heat. The dirty looks. The intentional-unintentional bumps in the hallway. The eye rolling, teeth sucking when I walked by and whispers too.

Camille told me it was because of Rahiem. I agreed. It also had something to do with the amount of attention that different guys had begun showing me too. Guys that I wasn't even the least bit interested in. Some who went to middle school with me, who I peeped in middle school but wasn't checkin for me in my tom-boy days. They would always be up in my face now. "Shawrty, wassup wit you? Can I call you sometime, Ma?" Funny how one summer could drastically change a person.

Algebra didn't look that hard; I wished the class would shut up long enough for me to get the full instructions. The short older man standing in front of the class reminded me of Mr. Magoo. Tarsha, a short, heavy set girl who set in front of me with a bad weave kept turning around talking to Kareem who was sitting next to me. They cracked jokes from the time we stepped foot in the class until it was over. Both of them had every class with me, every day. Kareem was a straight clown. I don't know why he felt the need to attention seek, as my Aunt Debbie would call it. His skin was black like coffee, no cream.

Kareem was smart. He spoke well, when he wanted to. I could tell he had manners and someone had instilled some respect and morals in him, even though he tried to pretend like a hoodlum. He dressed nice and always wore a watch. He dubbed himself Mr. Polo because he wore Polo shirts almost every day. Kareem didn't need to attention seek.

Tarsha on the other hand, her weave was always bad and her shoes always looked like they were screaming for help. She was loud, which I thought drew too much attention to her raggedy hair. She was mean too which I thought someone who was clearly less fortunate, shouldn't be. She was an easy target for guys to crack jokes on, and they did but never to her face. She hung with three other girls whom all looked like they shared their sibling's clothes. Their jeans were always dingy, shirts always brown around the neck and yellow under the arms.

"What kind of shoes are those? Them jawns nice!"

"Yo, you joe!" Tarsha piped at Kareem

Kareem hunched down to get a closer look at my coach sneakers that Leigh had got me. He slipped my sneaker right off my foot.

"Yo, these things is fresh." He smelled them and screwed his face all up like he smelled a foul odor. I jumped out my seat in attempt to grab my sneaker from him but stumbled over Tarsha's book bag. I almost fell on her but caught myself just in time. She jumped up before I had a chance to take a step back. Her face was nearly touching mine and her double D's were pressed firmly against my chest. My heart beat sped up.

"Damn yo! You all up on me and shit." A sprinkle of spit landed on my cheek. I just stood there, frozen in place. I could feel hundreds of eyes all piercing on me. People began to chant. "Fight, fight, fight!"

"Damn yo, Zhar she all up in ya shit. You gone let her invade ya space in shit? Everybody know you nice and shit wit ya gear let's see how that fight game is." Kareem piped in. The crowd grew louder. "Fight! Fight! Fight!"

"Now let's all take a seat now." Mr. Magoo sang out like a lullaby. I couldn't move. I didn't know if I should swing or just walk away. I had never fought before. Never had someone this bold and piped in my face. The teacher came over to us and put his hands between us to part us. Tarsha sat down first and then I stepped back and took my seat.

"Give me my damn shoe Kareem!" I snatched my shoe from Kareem but not before mugging him in the forehead.

"Let me see you mug Tarsha like that yo!"

"Man get the fuck outta here, you a fuckin instigator." Tarsha was sitting side ways. I guess she didn't want to have her back to me. Not that I planned to do anything. I slid my sneaker on and rested my feet in the wire basket under her chair. The class was still rowdy and trying to pipe us up. People were placing bets on who would win if we fought. The ten minutes that was left for that class was draggin it's ass as if it knew I was about to lose my cool. All kinds of emotions ran through my body. Mostly panic from being embarrassed. Just as the clock said three minutes to go, a spit ball flew from the back of the class and landed on the back of Tarsha's neck. It was huge and dripping with spit. The entire class erupted with laughter, including myself.

The pain in my face felt like a bee sting. It didn't hurt that bad but it caught me off guard. I had no time to gather my thoughts before I felt myself falling out my chair and my hair being pulled. Once I realized that I was in a fight, I was on the ground already and Tarsha was on top of me. She was heavy and I tried to roll her fat hundred and fifty pounds off of my little buck of five body. But she wasn't budging. I went to grab her weave but it came right out on the first pull. A voice in me kept screaming, "*get her off of me*". I wrapped my hands around her neck and furiously squeezed. I squeezed until my fingers touched. Making my fingers fit around her chubby neck was the goal. It took a few seconds but before I knew it, I felt her stop hitting me and struggling to get my fingers off her neck. I dug my nails down into her skin tighter and in the front where my thumbs were positioned I felt a little lump, I pushed it in as hard as I could. I remember hearing something on TV saying that you could cut off someone's air supply if you squeezed that tight enough.

As I became more conscious of my surroundings and what was going on, I could hear the crowd. I began to panic more because I knew everyone was watching me get beat up. Rage began to build in me. I hear the teacher screaming "security, security." He's trying to pull Tarsha off of me but I won't allow my hands to let go of her neck. I taste blood in my mouth. It's like a light bulb goes off in my head. The rage in me escapes the jail that it was locked in. I sprint to my feet, with Tarsha's neck still in my hands, vigorously squeezing.

"Bitch I will fucking kill you!" I hear the voice, but I don't recognize it. "I hate you bitch! I hate you!" Now I have two security guards pulling my fingers from Tarsha's neck. One of them slaps a hand cuff on one of my hands. It's like I wake up from a bad nightmare, unaware of what's going on. I hear the voice still screaming "die bitch!" It's my own voice. I am escorted to the dean's office in handcuffs.

"Ms. Washington," The dean had a folder in his hand with my last name and first initial on it. He sighed and looked up at me. "Why are you here?" He clasped his hands together? With my heart still racing, adrenaline racing through my veins doing a hundred, I said "because I was in a fight."

"No, why are you *here*? As in, Germantown?"

I rolled my eyes at the thought. "Because I didn't get accepted anywhere else!"

"But Ms. Washington, your grades are stellar; it looks like –in middle school."

"Yeah but-" I stopped. I didn't feel like telling this man my entire sob story. Besides, I begin to feel stinging on the back of my neck and the handcuffs are cutting into my skin. I thought about what Leigh was going to say. Probably not much now days. Shake her head maybe, if I could get her attention long enough.

"Ms. Washington, you need to do better. This kind of behavior will not be tolerated in my school."

"Can you take these off of me? I'm not a criminal. She attacked me. I was defending myself."

"I'm not going to call the cops and have you arrested this time. But if I see you in my office again for something like this, I will."

I was suspended for three days. It was Tuesday so I couldn't return to school until Monday. When I got home from school, news had already reached home. Leigh was doing hair on the porch and Nikki was standing in the doorway talking to this guy name Man who went to school with me and lived around the corner from us.

"So you let somebody beat you up?" Nikki barked as I walked up the steps. I said nothing. I walked past her and headed upstairs. Leigh called out behind me.

"You better get ya little ass down here."

"I have to go to the bathroom." I sat on the steps in our bathroom staring in the full length mirror. My face was still intact and un-bruised. But my neck looked like I was attacked by a hyena. My clothes were sloppy and stretched out of shape. The fight was nearly three hours ago and yet, my heart still raced. All I could hear was the voices of everyone who watched.

Damn, yo she got Zhar.
Zhar took a L.
Guess looks don't get you very far now Zhar.
It's always the badd jawns that can't fight!

I cried. The tears eased down my face as I felt rage dance within me. As my thoughts flashed back to the fight, they also flashed back to Cashay and the beatings my Aunt Bobbie use to give her. I thought about the time she was on top of Cash, banging her head against the floor. And the time she was washing my hair and I cried because the water was scalding hot as I lay with my head in the kitchen sink. The more I cried the harder she scrubbed my hair and the more I squirmed, ultimately I busted my lip on the sink. The taste of blood in my mouth as my scalp burned reminded me of the fight that day.

Dear Diary,
    I always wondered how this could be my life. Out of all the places in the world, all the people I could be born to. I always wonder why I was born to Katherine and Desmond. Why did I have to be born black and a girl? If I was white, my life wouldn't be like this. I wouldn't live in this part of the world, go to these kinds of schools, or have this kind of family. I swear I feel like I don't belong in this family. This can't be my life. I'm in this dumb school, way out of my comfort zone, learning new ways to live because nobody ever taught me about how to handle the hood and people who came from the hood. Funny thing is, the more and more I think about it, the hood has always been all around me, I just never had the pleasure of being able to touch it. All the summers that Aunt Debbie took us to Virginia Beach, AC, and kept us in Cheerleading, Girl Scouts, and dance class, what she was really doing was keeping us away from someone else's reality. She was keeping us away from the ignorance, the lack of respect, lack of self-worth, drive, and determination. Getting outside of Philly, driving down 95 South seeing the signs "Welcome to Delaware", "Welcome to Myrtle Beach, "Welcome to North Virgina", those signs made me feel like I could go anywhere, be anything. Being in Germantown makes me feel worthless, like a failure. I didn't get accepted to any of the good schools so I'm left to bullshit my way through high school-fighting, cussing, skipping class and learning to tune the teacher out. I thought school would be fun, enlightening, upbeat, encouraging, like Saved by the Bell or something. I don't see no pep rallies, debate teams, honor's society, or anything like that. They do have a ROTC program but I don't even know what that stands for. It looks like some kind of military program or something. I hope I don't have to stay in this school for too long. If I do, I think I may become just another statistic. Camille is getting transferred to Roxborough in a few weeks. I'm going to be so alone. Aunt Debbie says she knows someone at Nikki's school and looking into getting me transferred. I sure hope that happens this year.

The Monday I went back to school I didn't know how to act. I didn't know if I could continue walking around like my shit didn't stink, or if I should run and hide in the back of the class. That afternoon while I sat in the lunch room I heard that Tarsha had been expelled. She had already got suspended two times before that for fighting so they expelled her. While there were people still talking about the fight, it wasn't on blast like I thought it was. There had been at least six other fights since then that people were talking about now. I spotted Rahiem across the lunch room as I walked through with my new leather book bag and matching sneakers. Rahiem was in a circle of people, mostly his crew and some groupie chicks. I hadn't talked to Rahiem since the day before the fight. Leigh put me on punishment and took my phone privileges away until I got off suspension.

Rahiem notices me walking toward him and he seemed to look uncomfortable, nervous even. I approach with Camille beside me. Camille had become cool with almost everyone in the G. She has older brothers who went to the G and know a lot of guys who are still in the G. Camille is also very approachable. Her smile is bright and welcoming. Her energy is positive and vibrant. Not like me.

She's laughin and talkin loud. Poppin her neck and suckin her teeth every other curse word. Everybody seems to be eating her words right up. She's animated and full of energy. Taj and Reece, two of Rahiem's friends are smiling ear to ear at her. Her breast are bouncing in her two size too small GAP t-shirt. Her pudgy belly peeks out from the bottom, exposing a piercing. The laughter seizes.

"Ah yo, wassup Zhar, Camille." I nod at everyone. Camille waves. Reece embraces Camille with a bear hug. He has a thing for her but knows she has a boyfriend. Rahiem's eyes keep missing mine. He's darting back and forth to everyone but me. Lisa, I think her name is, sits down on the table and rest her feet on the bench part. She's sweating like she just ran a marathon.

"So yall chillin this lunch?" Reece breaks the silence.

"Nah, we just passin through. Some of us want to get our education this year." I say. The grin on my face expresses my sarcasm, something I've become accustom to hiding behind when I'm nervous. My pager vibrates. I pull it off my hip to check the number. I don't recognize it and wonder who it could be this time of morning.

"Ok, pimpin, we see you getting hit up and it ain't even noon yet." Reece is making conversation but something is off. The vibe feels weird. Rahiem has not even come over to me or acknowledged me. I feel uncomfortable. Did something happen between Rahiem and I, and I missed the memo?

"Never pimpin, I leave that all to you. We gotta go tho, we check yall later." I flash a flirty smile that misses Rahiem's eyes again because Lisa has his attention.

"Yo, did you see that?" Camille questions.

"How could I miss it?" I stop at the pay phone at the exit of the cafeteria and dial the number back.

Dear Diary,

I wonder where Kat is, if she thinks about me. I haven't heard from her since I came back home from Michigan. That was almost six months ago. I guess she really feels bad now. She should. I don't know what's wrong with her. Who just ups and leaves their children? Cash is having a baby. She's due any day now. Aunt Debbie gave her a nice baby shower. The father didn't come. I don't think she knows who the father is. I heard Aunt Debbie saying that Cash was a stripper and pregnant by one of her customers. I wanted to ask Cash where she's been all these years and why she never came back for me like she promised she would but she's different now. She's not the same Cash I remember. It's like she isn't even my sister anymore. The fights between Mike and Leigh are getting worse. Last night they were out front and all the neighbors were out there watching. I don't understand why Leigh stays with him. How can you claim to love someone and you push them down the steps, stalk them and jump out of closets on them? Is that love? I wonder how Leigh feels. She's changing. She used to be so wise and full of life. Uncle Tony is still on the run. Things have calmed down a little bit. They are in another house in Mt. Airy, their third place in two years. I wonder if Uncle Tony is thinking of a master plan or if he (we) will be on the run for the rest of our lives. Writing this makes me wonder if this is real life, or if this is a dream. I never thought life would be like this. I guess I never really thought about life being like anything except what I see on Family Matters or Full House. This is like a Mob movie though, unreal. I don't know what's going on with Rahiem. Something isn't right.

Rahiem's pager vibrated on the glass table. I didn't think twice before I picked it up to read it.

I dialed the number back. "Hello, someone page Rahiem?"

"This is Lisa, who it this?"

My lips were tightly pressed together. My thoughts raced as my once quick and sassy mouth seemed to be paralyzed at this moment.

"Lisa who?"

"Ah, where is Rahiem?" Her words were quick and piercing. Before I could gather my thoughts to respond, Rahiem walked in. The pain in my face was surely readable. I hadn't yet learned to control my facial expressions with Rahiem. I hit the off button on the cordless phone and laid it on the table. For what seemed like forever, we both remained silent.

Rahiem to tried to explain but there was no explaining the obvious. I had been seeing things and hearing things about Rahiem but I never had any real reason to indulge in the idea that Rahiem was cheating on me. That was until now. Now it all made since. Lisa, the girl with the too little GAP shirt and belly piercing from the lunch room. Her number was in Rahiem's pager over a dozen times, all times of the night.

My chest burned uncontrollably. I'm not sure if it was because the idea of Rahiem sleeping with someone else was unbearable that it burned holes in my heart or if the rage was beating and pounding so viciously inside of me -my poor heart took the beating as I caged the rage within. I held the tears in for dear life. I wouldn't allow one single tear to fall. *Crying is weak*, I repeated to myself.

"Azhar, please, listen, wait."

"Get off of me!" I pushed passed Rahiem with everything in me.

As I walked to the bus stop I allowed my thoughts to drift off and ponder Desmond. This was rare. But it was times like this where I wanted a dad. I wanted to call him and cry so hard about how my heart was shattered into a billion pieces. I wanted him to say some heartfelt words that would emphasize his love for me, his baby girl, and how he would place harm on anyone who hurt me. I wanted a protector, a savior, a father. I wanted a dad. I wanted my dad. But Desmond had never been any of those things to me. It had been years since I last seen him, four or five to be exact. In my mind his face was blurry because I barely remembered the features of the man who had forced Kat to bring me into this vicious world and abandon me like an unloved alley cat. A tear slid down my cheek. I brushed it aside quickly and erased the painful thoughts of Desmond.

The forty-five minute ride home allowed me to escape deeper into my thoughts. For the remainder of my ninth grade year Rahiem and I repeated the same vicious cycle. Break up, make up, I would cry, scream and fight random chicks who were either jealous of Rahiem's and I relationship, or intimidated by me. Three out of school suspensions that year, two in school, and a plethora of detentions, mostly un-served. Aunt Debbie was fed up with my behavior. I was fed up with life. The uncertainty of what tomorrow would bring weighed heavy on me.

CHAPTER 7

Clark High. Clark was one big melting pot. There were people of all races and nationalities here. My aggression grew daily. My first year at Clark I met tons of people, developed a reputation of being an *it* girl, fucked around and got suspended three times for fighting.

"That's her."

"Who?"

"The new girl. That's Nikki's little sister." The girl with the white eye makeup tried to whisper as I walked by.

The lunchroom was jammed pack. It wasn't as large as Germantown's lunchroom and it had much more diversity in it than Germantown ever had too. Diversity. I learned that word earlier that day in my Social Economics class. Clark also offered more than the basic English, Math and Science like Germantown did. Clark was a good school where you could study a trade. It was what they called a *special admit*. Meaning, you had to apply and go through a selection process which included an interview and stuff. Anyway, Aunt Debbie was good friends with someone who worked there and after such a horrible first year at Germantown, she was adamant that I transfer out before they kicked me out. I was happy to leave the G. Camille had transferred out midway through the year to another special admit school. Things just weren't the same when she left.

I walked to the end of the lunchroom and took a seat at a nearly empty table. I scanned the room. I didn't know one single person but people were looking at me as if they knew me.

"So you're Nikki's sister?"

"Azhar."

"Huh?" The girl with the white eye makeup questioned.

"My name is Azhar and I have a sister name Nikki."

"I'm Amber, and this is Keisha."

"Hey." I dryly said. I darted my eyes down at my pager. It was Rahiem.

"You cute." The girl who was introduced as Keisha stated. Her statement was so off topic, borderline sarcastic. I couldn't help but indulge.

"I know." I kept my eyes down, not making eye contact. Amber sucked her teeth and just as quickly as they walked up, they walked away.

I made it through the day without getting lost. I went to all my classes and told myself I was going to do better in this school. I actually was going to apply myself, do some quality work. Eighth period ended and everyone spilled out the doors into the streets. I caught up with Nikki at the Pizza store at the corner and we walked to the bus stop. There were nearly fifty kids waiting to get on the bus, so we walked up a few stops to make sure we would get on.

On the bus Nikki and I got separated. I made my way to the back of the bus and lucked up and got the last seat available. The double, stretch bus was jammed packed. As the bus began to move, a group of girls who were standing in front of me began to slap box. The bus was so loud, everyone was screaming, laughing obnoxiously and making all kinds of noises. I glanced around to see Amber and Keisha sitting a few seats down from me.

The closer the girls got to my fresh Pro Keds the more annoyed I became. I was mad that they decided to slap box on a crowded ass bus to begin with.

"Zhar you good?" Nikki called out to me from the front of the bus.

"Yeah, I'm good." I said sucking my teeth.

"She good!" Keisha yelled back to Nikki. I was shocked that Keisha knew Nikki. I shouldn't have been though, Nikki knew everyone. She was always the popular one. I was always just *Nikki's little sister*.

"Yo! Watch it." I blurted out after four times of ignoring the one girl who kept almost falling on me.

"Yo chill. It's not that deep." Her words were barely audible. Almost as if she wasn't sure she wanted to speak them out loud.

"But it is though!"

Other people begin to chime in, expressing their frustration with all the commotion they were causing but the two girls just ignored them and continued to push and shove one another. Before I knew it, the one girl was falling directly on top of me. I sprung to me feet forcing her to fall to the floor. The bus erupted in laughter. Her embarrassment spread across her face instantly.

"Damn! What the fuck?" I yelled.

The doors to the bus flew open.

"Last stop. Everybody off!" The bus driver called out. I shot one last dirty look down at her before stepping over her and exiting the bus.

Bitch, I mouthed as our eyes locked.

I could hear people clowning her as I walked away. I checked my sneakers when I hit the sidewalk. The black scuff was large across the top, ruining them. I was disgusted. I waited patiently for Nikki to get off the bus. I kept glancing over at the crowd that was forming around the girls who were on the bus. I caught sight of Nikki pushing her way off the bus.

"Soon as she get off the bus you better hit her. Just steal the shit out of her." Nikki coached.

The crowd began to move quickly toward me and as soon as my eyes locked in on my target, I swung. My hand landed heavily on her cheek and I positioned my other hand on her head and took hold of a handful of hair and held her in position.

"That's right Zhar get her!"

Her wild swings were landing on my back. I swung her around by her hair causing her to fall to the grown. I jumped on top on her as the crowd cheered on. The more the crowd cheered, the more adrenaline I felt running through my body. Before I knew it, I was banging her head against the ground.

"Five Oh, Five Oh!" A voice called out.

"Come on Azhar!" The crowd began to scatter. The sirens got louder as the cop cars got closer. Nikki and I both ran to the subway. Under the sub on the train, every face is a kid from school. Everyone is yelling and telling recounts of the story and even acting out their rendition of what happened. The adrenaline is still power walking through my body. My heart beat hasn't slowed yet and I think it's partly because of everyone's else's energy.

"Yo you fucked that girl up little Nikki."

"Yea, she did. That was so crazy!" Everyone agreed.

"But my name is Azhar!" I inserted my voice into all the chaos. All eyes were on me. Nikki stood by the door in between two guys from the football team.

"Oh-kay, cool! Got it. Azhar didn't even make it through her first day without a fight. We got a little beast on our hands." Kyree announced, causing everyone to explode into laughter. His smile was contagious. He was standing on top of the seats looking down at everyone just as someone began to drop a beat on the window. Just then someone else joined in on the beat. Before I knew it, the entire train had began adding some type of noise to this beat where Kyree begin to rap in a Jamaican accent, chanting my name in between bars.

"Don't call her Nikki, cause that girl real vicious and her attitude get real shitty." Kyree called out over the beat.

"Did you see the legs on that girl, hey alley cat, her walk so mean, she probably got a fat little kitty." The entire train erupted. I couldn't hold back my laughter anymore.

The morning of my first day at Clark, I had no idea I'd be in a fight and gain so much attention. I had prepared to be the new girl for the first three or four months, sitting at lunch by myself, walking to class getting lost and feeling out of place until I became a familiar face and people began to notice me. But that was hardly the case. People knew my name like we were from the same hood but we weren't. I didn't know any of these people, just Nikki and our cousin Kia.

Nikki and I didn't tell Aunt Debbie or anyone that I was fighting. This was supposed to be my fresh start since I did so horribly in Germantown the year before.

The next morning Nikki and I headed to school. Once inside, she went her way to her classes and I climbed the steps to the fifth floor to my locker. Keisha and Amber stood in front of my locker laughing and talking with Kyree and a few other boys.

"Yo, that girl- what's her name Amber?" Keisha began as soon as she saw me approaching.

"Shalena, I think." Amber answered. Amber was thin, tall and wore colorful eye shadows that not everybody could. She dressed nice and her hair was always on point.

"Yeah, Shalena" Keisha continued. "Her and her brother are looking for you. I think they gone try to jump you-"

"But we got you so don't worry." Kyree interjected.

"Man, it's whatever." I turned the combination lock a few times and pulled it open. I shoved some books in it. "So, what she mad she got her ass beat yesterday?" I slowly cut my eyes as I heard Nikki's voice coming around the corner. I could hear the tone in her voice escalating which wasn't good. There was another voice that I didn't recognize and a guy's voice too. I slammed my locker and ran towards Nikki's voice. Keisha, Amber and the rest of their crew ran behind me.

Nikki was nose to nose with this boy while Kia tried to stand in between them. The bell rang as I reached Nikki and students from every class spilled into the hall. Nikki kept yelling. Her hand was inches from the boy's face. Shalena was standing behind her brother and with two more girls. Nikki caught sight of me, gave me the look and all hell broke lose. Nikki finger pointing turned into fist throwing. That boy didn't even know what hit him. I followed up punching him in the head and face until he fell to the grown. I could hear chants, *fight, fight, fight, fight*. I jumped to my feet and me and Nikki went crazy stomping and kicking him all over.

"Break it up! Break it up!" School security called out. I caught sight of Kia and Keisha fighting Shalena. Security escorted us to the office where my heart was beating fast but no out of fear. The office was packed. Keisha, Kia, Nikki, Amber, Kyree and four other boys that was with Kyree. The boys were in handcuffs.

"Yo, what the fuck happened?" I whispered to Keisha. She seemed to be in charge of her crew. This was my first time really paying her any attention. She was about my height, a little thicker than me and about my complexion. Her face was clear of makeup and her style was simple. Jeans, t-shirt and Jordans. Her demeanor was stern.

"When you and Nikki jumped Corey, Shalena tried to jump in it so we jumped them. Yo, ya cousin Kia is bout it!"

Kia wasn't our blood cousin. She was one of my Aunt Debbie's friend's daughter but we had been friends since we were young so we just called her our cousin. She attended all our family functions and came over for dinner sometimes too.

"Azhar Washington and Nigera Jones." The tall thin man with the bald head called out to us. We followed him into the small office.

"Take a seat." His demeanor said he was tired, warn out but once he proceeded to speak, the smell of liquor on his breath told me he was drunk or hung-over. "It is only two weeks into school and hear you are starting a riot in my school. Miss Washington, this is only your second day of school with us. What is wrong with you?" His words dragged.

"I-"

"No, I did not give you permission to speak."

I darted my eyes down feeling like my Uncle Tony was scalding me. My eyes rested on the name plate on the brown desk. Terrence Malone, it read. "I do not tolerate this kind of behavior. I know your mother. I know her very well too."

You don't know my mother, I thought. "Oh really?" I challenged.

"Yes, Debra and I are old friends. We go way back." He smirked, as if his mind had escaped to a more happier time. He began to smile really hard. He licked his lips slowly.

"Do you know my father too?" Nikki quizzed. His eyes blinked rapidly.

"Ah, um. Yeah. Yes. Yes, I know your father."

"Good!"

I couldn't suppressed my smile. *Good one Nikki.* "Mr. Malone, we ain't start no riot!"

"Didn't. It's we didn't start a riot." He corrected. I rolled my eyes. I knew the correct way to speak. But everybody talked like that and when I spoke correctly, people looked at me like the crazy one.

"You're correct." I agreed.

"Look, I'm suspending you. I have to. I won't expel you which is would I would normally do in this case. This is a good school! This is not your neighborhood school and we are not babysitters. Kids come here to learn and we are here to teach and educate. If that is not what you are here for then, this is not the place for you. Now, Nigera this is your first offense so I'm just going to give you three days, but Azhar, you have been suspended multiple times in your previous school and Debra assured me that you would not be a problem. What's going on? What's a beautiful, smart girl like you doing getting into all these fights, and don't tell me people are jealous of you. I don't want to hear that." Mr. Malone sat back in his chair with his hands clasped together waiting for me to respond. I didn't. I rolled my eyes and leaned back in my chair. What difference did it matter? He didn't care about me and I didn't care to tell him that with each fight I felt a small sense of relief from the rage that I tried to silence.

"Okay, Azhar, I am suspending your for a week. You must return with a parent."

"Fine."

"Wait, your parent has to come and get you."

"Great, just fuckin great." Nikki mumbled. We called Leigh instead of my Aunt. She came to get us and promised not to tell my Aunt Debbie.

CHAPTER 8

"I don't know what kind of slick stuff yall thought yall were pulling calling Leigh instead of me." Aunt Debbie was flaming mad. I don't know what me and Nikki thought we were doing either. Ever since Aunt Debbie and Nikki had moved back in, the house was over crowded, and my Aunt Debbie was always in bitch mode. My Uncle Tony was, I don't know where. He always moved around these days. The cops still followed me and Nikki to school too.

"Mom, we didn't do anything. We were just defending ourselves." Nikki insisted.

"Shut up! Yall never doing anything. It's never your fault. It's always somebody else. I'm sick of this shit. The fighting, the cutting class, the boys, the late night phone calls. Don't think I don't hear that phone ringing all hours of the night either. Yall getting too damn grown."

I never argued with my Aunt Debbie. She was the type of person that no matter how right you were she would try to convince you that you were wrong. There was no winning any arguments. I think my Uncle knew that too because I never heard them argue. Anytime my Aunt would get upset, and raise her voice, my Uncle would stop talking. He would let her say whatever and eventually she would stop talking. But not Nikki. Nikki was bullheaded and went toe to toe with my Aunt Debbie. Eventually, Nikki would be forced to back down only because my Aunt would threaten to have my Uncle beat her. We all knew he wouldn't literally beat her with a belt at this age but Nikki always backed down at that point.

"Azhar, you are out of control! You are not even sixteen yet. I pulled a lot of strings for you to get into this school. You better stop following behind Nikki cause she has to answer to her father."

I never understood when my Aunt would say this, as if I didn't have to answer to him too. I mostly tried not to deal with my Aunt these days. I

60

tried to only talk to Leigh but since Aunt Debbie was back home, I barely saw Leigh.

My week long suspension dragged it's ass. I stayed in my room most of the day writing in my journal, thinking. I thought a lot. I thought about Kat mostly. She was on my mind heavy. I couldn't shake it. Her voice, her scent, her smile. I dreamed about her too. Mostly bad dreams, nightmares about her being murdered in a crack house. All the dreams seemed so real. The smell of burned glass, her screams, the fear in her eyes, it all seemed touchable in my dreams. The more I thought about Kat, the angrier I became.

Dear Diary,

I don't know what's wrong with Aunt Debbie. She's always so snappy. I think everything with Uncle Tony is worrying her. She keeps trying to make it seem like I'm doing all this stuff like Nikki isn't doing the same stuff. Something is up with Nikki. She's acting weird, distant. Rahiem, well, he's Rahiem, still cheating. Camille told me he is messing with some girl name Crystal. She's light skinned and wears a weave. I can't wait to go back to school. I like Clark. It's different than Germantown. I don't know how to explain it. People there are so interested in me, Azhar.

"What is wrong with you?" I was tired of pretending that I didn't notice a change in Nikki. Our relationship was different now. Before I went to Michigan we were inseparable, now all she wanted to do was hangout with her boyfriend and go to the shop with Leigh. I don't know what could have happened in just the two weeks that I was gone. Our two year age difference never was an issue before but now it seemed like Nikki was acting like I was too young to hangout with her. She was driving now and was getting a Tahoe for Christmas if her grades were good -so maybe the driving thing gave her leverage.

"Nothing, why you say that?"

"You're acting different."

"What do you mean different?" Nikki pulled her t-shirt over her head and sat on the edge of the bed.

"I don't know. Just different." I wanted to just blurt out how unattached from her I felt now but I knew I would get emotional and Nikki was like her mother; emotionless. I had never seen Nikki cry, just like I had never seen my Aunt Debbie cry. Their lack of emotions and scalding of me when I cried forced me to hide my tears and hold them for the shower. I suppressed them all the time but the relief I felt from the cutting, man, that was better than crying. I was happy that I hadn't yet left any scars but I knew what I was doing was crazy. I just had to figure out how to release the anger and frustration without cutting or crying.

"Hey, Azhar, come sit with us." Keisha called as I walked into the lunchroom. It was my first day back to school. Aunt Debbie was so mad at me, I got my phone privileges taken and my pager taken. I was glad to be out the house and in school. "We going downtown after school today, you wanna go?" It was about five boys sitting at the table, Keisha, Amber and two other girls I didn't know. I sized everyone up. We all had on nice gear; except one girl. Her Keds were run over and her jeans were fading on the seams. Keisha hair was on point, she had a pager and her nails were fresh. Amber was tight with her makeup and her clothes were fresh too. The boys all had on fresh sneakers, most of them in Jordans, jeans and t-shirts. Everybody was talking to me like they had knew me for years. I don't know why but I liked them.

We headed downtown after school that day. We ended up on South Street. Keisha kept talking to me. She was a straight shooter.

"So you and Nikki sisters? Yall don't look a like. Are you real sisters?"

"Real like we came out the same pussy. Is that real enough?" I spit back. I think Keisha was use to being in charge and people backing down. She had met her match.

"Oh, that's cool. All the dudes like her." Keisha wasn't saying nothing I didn't already know.

"Yeah cause she got a fat ass." Kyree said smacking hands with another one of the boys that was with us. "She got all the ass, what you got?" He walked around me as if he needed to look at me from every angle. All eyes were on me.

"I got a box game out this world. I know you seen it!"

"Ok, ok. We good." Kyree through his hands up in the air to signal he didn't want any problems.

"I bet we good."

"You cute though. You ain't got a dunk like yah sister but you cute."

The train ride home was crazy. We laughed and joked the entire ride. When I finally got home it was after six o'clock. It was getting dark. I walked in the house to see my Aunt Debbie sitting on the couch with Nikki and Leigh.

"Where have you been?"

"I went downtown afterschool." I sat the three bags down.

"What part of punishment don't you understand?" Aunt Debbie asked.

"I didn't know I was still on punishment."

"Did I tell you that you were off punishment?"

"No but you said a week. It's been a week." I took off my jacket and laid it across the chair. Before my Aunt had a chance to respond, Leigh spoke up. "Azhar, you were on the phone last night until like two in the morning."

"I was not on the phone! I was sleep by like ten o'clock."

"There you go rolling your eyes and raising your voice. Who do you think you're talking to?" My Aunt always swore I had a problem rolling my eyes. She swore that I was always being disrespectful by the tone in my voice. I never figured out how to tell her that the change in the tone in my voice came from me suppressing the tears. The lump in my throat would raise and I'd fight for dear life not to cry.

"Aunt Debbie, I'm not raising my voice." I took slow, deep breaths. "I was not on the phone last night or any this week. Nikki was." Nikki's face shot to beat red. I usually was the blame for everything. Nobody ever suspected that Nikki was doing anything. Not that she was hiding anything, they just never got on her like they got on me.

"We aren't talking about Nikki. That's your problem, you are always so worried about other people. You need to worry about Azhar." I knew there was no getting out of this. I just kept quiet. I let my Aunt Debbie and Leigh talk for the next twenty minutes. They talked about all kinds of nothing. Well, not nothing but shit that was old and not even worth listening to. A boy that I liked two summers ago and they read a letter he had wrote to me saying how he wanted to finger me. I don't understand why they were mad at me. It wasn't like we had sex or I wrote it to him. Leigh mentioned Rahiem and all the drama I had going on with the different girls he was dealing with. Still, I don't know why they were mad at me.

"And this new guy, what's his name Nikki? Kareem?" Leigh quizzed. My heart beat sped up. *Shit! How did they know about Kareem?* Kareem, just thinking about him made me smile. Kareem was twenty five. Ten years older than me, two years younger then Leigh. I met Kareem one day I was with Nikki. We were walking in the mall and this guy walks up to Nikki and introduces his self to us as Fats. He was heavy set, so I guess the name Fats was accurate. He had a full beard, bald head, and smelled like heaven. His scent was intoxicating. Fats was twenty nine. Him and Nikki started kickin it heavy and the summer of my ninth grade year he introduced me to Kareem. Kareem was from North Philly. Light skinned, wavy hair, grey eyes with a full beard. Kareem and Fats were street niggas. Hustlers, drug dealers, but not corner boys. Kareem never told me the ins and outs of what he did but I know he was making runs out New York and Pittsburgh for Fats. He was always on the road but when he made time for me, I enjoyed every second. Kareem wasn't the first older guy that I had talked to but he was the first one I felt like I was falling for. I knew between his age and what he did, I had to keep him a secret. Kareem was the one who brought me my pager and paid the bill for it every month. When we would hook up, he would always have a gift for me. Sometimes sneakers, or a card with money. It would be anywhere between a hundred to two hundred dollars. He said he didn't know how to shop for a female so he started getting me gift cards to Victoria's Secret, BeBe, Gap, and Saks. The first few times we saw each other we didn't have sex. He just wanted me to chill with him. He would smoke and watch TV and I would do my homework. He always told me that he didn't want me to feel pressured to have sex with him and that if I wanted to leave at anytime, I could. I never wanted to.

"I don't know." Nikki answered. Nikki wasn't going to say anything about Kareem because then that would give up Fats.

"It's Kareem. I'm sure that's what he said. He sounds like a grown ass man! He calls all day while you're in school, so I know he must be out of school." I sat silently. I ignored the uncomfortable silence. This is becoming the norm. The un-comfortableness.

"You don't have anything else to say." My Aunt Debbie asked.

I try not to roll my eyes. "No. Can I go to my room now?" My Aunt signals with her hand for me to go upstairs. I grab my bags.

"Where you getting all this money from to buy all this stuff? You ain't been at the shop working?"

"Rahiem." I don't stop to look at Leigh as I answer her. In my room I take out the clothes I had just brought. I splurged a little bit spending three hundred dollars because Keisha brought a pair of BeBe Jeans that were a hundred and eighty dollars. Kareem had given me a two hundred dollar gift card the last time I had seen him. I hoped that he would give me cash the next time I saw him. Seeing the new clothes excited me. Always having money in my pocket, not having to ask anyone for anything, it felt good. When I lived with Aunt Bobbie all I ever had was Nikki's too small clothes. I never got anything new of my own.

When my birthday or Christmas came around, I brought my own gifts. I didn't wait for anyone to buy me anything because that would never happen. I had learned that I was responsible for me very quickly.

I remember Christmas at my Aunt Bobbie's house was never all that great. We had a tree and two or three gifts a piece max. The one year right before I moved in with Aunt Debbie, Cash and I woke up to nothing. Not one single gift. There were gifts for my Aunt Bobbie's female friends and gifts that Crystal and Christine had brought for Aunt Bobbie, but nothing for Cash and I.

"You just better be lucky you eating." Aunt Bobbie barked at us, even though we didn't even dare ask about not having any gifts. I guess our facial expressions said it all.

The following year at Aunt Debbie's house Christmas was big. There were tons of gifts from Leigh to her children and Aunt Debbie and Uncle had brought their grandchildren so many gifts our entire living room was filled with gifts. Everyone had something. Everyone else more than me but I took my gifts and smiled. *If your own mother don't even buy you anything, you better be happy for this*, I would remind myself of this whenever I felt myself feeling disappointed.

Flashes of Kat and I standing in the middle of Broad Street one year flashed in my head.

"Azhar, go ask the nice people if they can spare some change." Kat pulled lent out of my hair , licked the tips of her fingers and wiped the corners of my eyes. "Go head baby. We have to eat."

"Can you spare some change, please?" Some people dug deep into their pockets and purses and gave me whatever quarters, nickels, dimes or pennies they had while Kat sat on the curb watching from a distance. When my little jacket pockets were full, I'd walk over to Kat and she would empty them and send me back across the street.

"Ms. Can you spare some change please?"

"How old are you?"

I put five fingers up, displaying my dirty nails and the hole in the sleeve of my jacket.

"Five?"

The lady seemed so surprised. "Where's your parents?" She demanded.

I tried to force words out but I was too scared to admit that the lady sitting across the street on the curb smoking the cigarette was my mom. Her eyes darted back and forth trying to spot my parents. I looked at the grown trying not to look over at Kat. Tears escaped the corners of my eyes.

"Are you hungry? Do you have a house?" She bent down kneeling on one knee in her sheer stockings and shinny shoes. "Are you okay?" She lifted my chin up.

I pushed these images out of my head and pulled out my journal. I had tons of fragmented images embedded in my head. Memories as young as three and four years old. I didn't remember full situations. Sometimes it would be just an image, or the sound of something, someone's voice or a scent. Scents, scents always sparked memories for me. Cigarette's always reminded me of Kat. She smoked religiously. The smell of beer reminded me of Desmond. If I didn't know any better I would have thought that was the scent of his cologne.

CHAPTER 9

"So what are you going to do?" Keisha and I were walking to class, it was mid-school year.

"I don't know. You think I should talk to him?"

"Yeah, why not?"

"I don't know. I can barely keep up with everyone I'm talking to now." I admitted. "Rahiem, Kareem, Sean, Amir, and what's the Barber name?"

"Girl please. Put them in rankings and prioritize them."

"Like organize them?"

"Ah, yeah!"

"Keisha, I can't talk to one more person. My pager never stops going off. I have to turn it off at night time because its non-stop." I laughed out loud but I was dead serious.

"You could be ugly and guys not like you at all."

"It's just too much."

"Azhar shut up. What you mean it's too much. You sound stupid."

I sucked my teeth. "Man, whatever." *Easy for you to say, you only talk to two people.*

"Let's go see who's in the lunchroom."

"Okay," I agreed. "But I can't stay, I have to get to this World History class."

"I'm leaving to go to the doctors after lunch."

"To the doctors for what?"

"To get my depo shot. You not on birth control?" Keisha quizzed. "Yall use condoms every time?" Her facial expression looked like she was confused even though I hadn't even answered the question.

"I use condoms with Rahiem sometimes. Most of the times. Kareem and I only had sex twice and we used a condom both times." I admitted.

"What about the rest?"

"The rest?" I asked. "The rest of who?"

"Azhar, come on. You only having sex with Rahiem and Kareem?"

"Yea! Who else you think I'm having sex with?" We walked into the lunch room and scanned it for a few seconds. I saw Nikki sitting at the back of the lunch room with the football team. As usual, I heard her before I saw her. Keisha and I spotted our crew at the same time.

"What about Tre?"

I smiled uncontrollably. "Nah, I ain't fuck him." My mind danced around as I thought about Tre. Tre was from Uptown. He was a corner boy. Keisha knew him and his brother because they lived around the corner from her. I had met Tre one day I was waiting on the bus stop outside Keisha house. His light skin, jet black curly hair and bright pink lips hypnotized me from the moment I saw him. His bowed legs reminded me of Rahiem. Tre was eighteen. He always reminded me that I didn't seem like I was only fifteen.

He had a two year old daughter and had a car. He offered to drive me home the day I met him, but I declined. Keisha filled me in about him and his baby momma drama he had going on later that night. Tre and I mainly played phone tag. When I would call him, he would be in the streets, hustling. When he would call or page me, it would be like two in the morning.

"You better get on that. He is one to fuck wit! He get a couple dollars." Keisha was always trying to get me on guys who got money. I wasn't really checkin for nobody money though. Rahiem gave me money when I asked. Kareem gave me money on a regular, and I still worked at the shop some days when Leigh needed. I could easily bring home a hundred dollars in one day.

I took a seat at our usual table and it quickly filled up. Amber came and sat across from me. She began her speed race talking with her overly bubbly voice as always. She browed the room and talked about everyone her eyes landed on. I watched her, silently. I was trying to understand her insecurities. People like her always amazed me. She was very pretty, her parents were married, they lived in a nice home in Cheltenham which was the wealthy section of Philly. She was all into church and whatnot being as though both her parents were pastors. I didn't get it. Every day she talked about any and everybody from their hair, to their clothes, to if their teeth were yellow or not. I once read a magazine article that said people like her deflect to keep the attention off them because they have severe low self-esteem and insecurities.

"Amber, are you on birth control?" I couldn't take not one more second of her rambling on about who was ugly or had on the wrong season shirt.

She darted her eyes between Keisha and I. "Yeah, why?"

"She's not on any!" Keisha's tone was loud. I'm sure deliberately.

"Are you fuckin crazy?" Amber was being dramatic slamming her hand down on the table. "You tryna get pregnant?"

"She crazy ain't she?"

I had never thought about birth control before. I had never had anyone talk to me about birth control, or condoms, or sex, nothing. Once when Leigh was talking to Nikki and I, she said "you better not be giving out no free pussy." That was the extent to our sex conversation.

I went and got a depo shot that day. It was a form of birth control that you only needed to take every six months. Keisha said she had been getting it ever since eighth grade. We just walked right in Planned Parenthood, filled out some registration forms, sat and waited to be called. I got a pregnancy test and tested for STDs. They even offered to give me a HIV test. I declined.

CHAPTER 10

Whatever demons you have, you will have to face them one day. You can run and hide, but eventually they will catch up to you. For my family, we all faced them together this warm Friday evening as Nikki left for her senior prom. Our house was jammed packed with at least forty adult family members, and twenty plus children under the age of eighteen, including myself, and Rahiem. Our neighbors were in and out of our house for plates of food and taking pictures of Nikki and her beautiful prom dress that was handmade with some expensive fabric she had brought from South Street. Because our family was well known, practically the entire block was outside enjoying the scenery as the stretch hummer pulled up in front of our house. Music was pumping from one neighbor's window, the street was jammed packed with cars double parked on both sides, kids were running up and down the block playing tag and eating dollar water ice from the corner store.

My Aunt Debbie and Uncle Tony was extremely proud of Nikki. You could see their excitement on their faces. I hadn't seen my Uncle Tony in a few months and was happy that everyone was there celebrating together. My cousin's Crystal and Christine had drove up from Jersey and my Aunt Bobbie was there with her girlfriend too. Leigh and Mike sat around drinking and laughing, enjoying the family time as if we all had no worries. Life was good. In this very moment, I loved my life. I loved the picture of my family in this very moment. We were happy. There was joy and genuine happiness in the air.

The moment the stretch hummer pulled off the block, everyone flooded back into our house, filling each room to capacity. It was loud with everyone talking and laughing and those who were intoxicated were even louder and more animated. Suddenly, twenty five plus men dressed in all black with white letters FBI painted across their backs, guns drawn in full force swept through our house snatching every male up and forcing them to the grown. Men in black came from every which way, our front door, back door, and basement. The women and children were escorted out of the house after all the men were removed. We stood outside in a straight line that lined the entire block, on display for the world to watch.

As I was one of the last out of the house, I proceeded down the steps and I caught a glimpse of Rahiem's face and what seemed like hundreds of people looking from their steps and windows. My heart dropped. This, this was the only piece of my life that I had never revealed to anyone, not even Rahiem. I couldn't ever bring myself to add more craziness onto all the other craziness I had already confided in Rahiem. But here, in this very moment, he and the rest of the world saw me and my family for who we were. Criminals.

Everybody stood silently outside with their hands on top of their heads like a scene in a movie or some shit. It wasn't real to them but to me, this was my life. Nikki and I had been living this, silently for the past two years. We were being followed to school and home. Our phones were tapped and we weren't allowed to let anyone know where we lived when we moved. Three houses in two years. We weren't allowed to give our phone numbers out or mention my Uncle Tony's name. I heard people whispering that they had the wrong house or that it was mistaken identity. But I knew better. I knew they were here for my Uncle. The thing I didn't know, was why. My Aunt Debbie kept her mouth sealed when it came to why we were on the run. I knew it had something to do with plated cars, identity theft and I thought I overheard a conversation about a murder in California that took place long before I was even born but I can't be sure.

One hour. That's how long it took the FBI to finally leave our home. My Aunt Debbie did her best to mask her humiliation and save face with the family, friends and neighbors but I knew she was dying inside. Leigh showed not one ounce of emotion. Not one. When the boys in black finally cleared out and we were allowed to talk to one another Leigh told me that my Uncle Tony got away just in time out the back door.

"Mike saw them setting up when he came back from the market with the ice while Nikki was still getting dressed." She whispered.

I had been sitting inside with Rahiem while Nikki got dressed. It was so much commotion going on and so many people in and out, I was just happy we were all under one roof. I had let my detective eye down. My Aunt Debbie had been preparing us for the past two years to be on the look-out for anything suspicious and for the most part I always watched my surroundings, especially when in our neighborhood. On this day though, I was too relaxed. I thought about my Uncle Tony. He was such a handsome man, strong, stern, and ruled. When he spoke, we all listened. Together him and my Aunt Debbie were a team. He was the head of the house but surely she was the neck.

That night, I didn't sleep not one second. Rahiem stayed way past midnight. I cried and cried until my eyes were so swell they barely could open. Rahiem just held me. We didn't talk at all. We just sat on the couch in silence other than my sobs.

I tossed and turned all night waiting patiently for Nikki to come home. She didn't. The next morning, nobody spoke about our house getting raided or even where my Uncle Tony was. We weren't silent but it was life a usual. Leigh and I went to the shop and Mike went to work. They didn't fight that night which was music to my ears. I don't think my little heart could stand anymore torture.

I called Rahiem and made arrangements to meet him at his house. He was home alone when I arrived. I headed to his room and stripped out of my clothes immediately.

"What time will your mom be home?" I asked.

"She's out with my Aunt. I don't know."

I searched the room with my eyes for a clock. The red lights read 8:34PM.

"Make love to me. Please." The room fell silent.

Rahiem and I had been together for two years. He was the one person on earth that knew me. Not the pretty dark skin girl with long hair. Not Nikki's little sister, or Azhar who dressed nice or anything that people thoughtlessly labeled me as. Rahiem knew my fears, my goals and aspirations, he saw me in every state possible. When I was happy and laughed uncontrollably, the ugly scars from my cutting, the eczema patches that invaded my body every winter and above all else, Rahiem knew my heart. He knew just how vulnerable I really was. He knew because he saw the scars of me being weak, he saw the tears when I couldn't handle it anymore, he saw it all. And he still loved me. He didn't give up and leave me like Kat and Desmond did, he didn't push me away when I was acting crazy or when things got tough like my Aunt Debbie did, he didn't turn his back on me like Cash. No matter what Rahiem and I went through and we went through a lot-he was always there for me. He was my one constant.

CHAPTER 11

Just two weeks after the raid on our house I found myself bagging up my clothes and moving in with Cash. A simple conversation between Nikki and I turned into a full blown argument that resulted in my Aunt Debbie butting in and imposing her wrong as usual opinion on to the subject. She said she didn't like my tone and honestly, I'm sure she didn't because as of late, she didn't like anything or anyone. She was arguing and fussing with everyone. Her and Leigh were constantly at war about the house not being clean or Leigh doing hair in the house, or Leigh and Mike coming and going all times of the night. The living arrangements were getting to be unbearable. When she wasn't fussing at Leigh she was picking with Nikki and every time I saw her coming my way, I'd head in the opposite direction. Aunt Debbie talked in circles and didn't care if nothing she said made sense or not, it was her house so it was law. So on this particular day, her word was the last word and she didn't want to hear anything I had to say. But I said it anyway.

"You know Azhar, I don't have to put up with this mess. If you think you're grown and want to do whatever you want, and say whatever you want, you can leave. I'm not going to deal with this mess."

I called Rahiem to help me take my things to Cash's apartment. This wasn't the first time my Aunt Debbie wasn't "going to deal with this mess." My eighth grade year she had put me out and I went to stay with Leigh for the summer but some how ended back up at Aunt Debbie's house the following school year.

Living with Cash was short lived, I didn't even bother to learn her address. I knew after the third day there, when we got into a fist fight because she put her feet on me that it wasn't going to last long. Cash was five years older than me but acted more like the baby sister than I did. Cash wanted to be the cool big sister so she would allow Rahiem to come over and spend the night with me. She gave me condoms and said "don't do anything I wouldn't do." I didn't like this Cash. I didn't know this Cash. She spent her nights at the strip club where she worked and spent her days sleep while I took my two year old niece to school with me.

By the time school had let out, I didn't know how I was going to make it through the summer living with Cash. It was fun some days hanging out with Cash and her dad's daughter Star who also lived with us. Star was older than cash by five years and was the real parent of the house. Some days Cash would be cool and other days she would have mood swings like my Aunt Bobbie and be flipping out or hiding in her room all depressed. Most of her worries was about money. It was always about money. Her and Star argued about money all the time. It seemed that Cash never had her half of the rent or part of a bill or something. I didn't understand how they spent so much time at work and going to parties to dance but never had any money.

That summer I ran away from Cash's house. It was only supposed to be a temporary thing for like two days until Star came back off her trip to Miami. Star was the only one who could talk some sense into Cash.

Cash was totally out of control. She was taking this big sister thing too far. She thought she could tell me what to do and whatnot which would have been cool except that it was kind of hard to take her serious when one minute she's giving me lessons on how to suck dick and the next she's telling me I have a curfew of 8:30pm because she has a date.

I called Rahiem but he wasn't home so I took the bus to Fats house hoping that Kareem would be there. He wasn't. Fats let me spend the night in his daughter's room and in the morning he told me that my Uncle Tony had called looking for me and that Nikki was really upset that I had involved Fats.

"Azhar, I can't have this kind of drama here. You know the kind of business I'm into -so my house gotta stay low. I can't have ya Uncle coming here wit no cops." Fats dug in his pocket and pulled out a fist full of money. He pulled off two, one hundred dollar bills. "I know Kareem would take care of you. He up state so I got you. Go to the mall, walk this off and then take your ass home."

I went to the mall, got something to eat and brought a pair of sneakers. I made a call to my Aunt Carmen's house which was Desmond's sister. She was the only one of all his sisters and brothers that I remembered. She didn't live to far from my Aunt Debbie when I was growing up and she would come visit me sometimes over the years. I had just recently ran into her downtown and got her number.

I explained to her what was going on and she gave me her address and told me to come to her house, and that she would take care of all of it. I took the long ride out South Philly to her apartment.

Once I got to my Aunt Carmen's house she was so happy to see me. I caught her up on my life since I was five years old, or at least the important parts. She mostly asked about Kat though. I didn't tell her she was HIV positive though. Rahiem was the only person I had confided in about that. Besides, my Aunt Carmen had enough information to paint Kat to be this monster already, she didn't need anymore.

"Yeah cause ya mom was something else." She sipped her Pepsi. "Her and your dad was a mess but your dad did the best he could with Kitty."

I tried to refrain from rolling my eyes as my Aunt Carmen gave me her unsolicited opinion about Kat. "Kat, man, she was beautiful, I remember. I was just a   child but I remember how bad she had your father wrapped around her little finger." She made a twirling motion in the air with her pointer finger. "He did anything your mother told him to do. He was a good man. He just got caught up with the wrong one." She filed her nails in between puffs on her cigarettes. "Have you heard from your dad since he got out of jail?"

I rolled my eyes. "You mean Desmond?"

"Your father!" She barked.

"Desmond." I laughed. "Desmond is not my father." I leaned back and crossed my legs. Carmen, yes, Carmen must not have realized who she was talking to. It had been years since her and the Washington's were in my life but surely they had to realize that I was not the innocent, naïve five year old *Doll Baby* as they called me from ten years ago.

"Girl I don't know who you think you talking to. You don't disrespect your father like that. He may have his faults but that Kitty, she is to blame for your father. She destroyed him. She destroyed us." She leaned up in her chair closer to me. "You know your mother slept with your Uncle.? She tried to whisper with her teeth clenched together but the anger in her tone made it impossible. "She's the reason your father killed his own brother, you hear me?" She asked as if I some how went deaf. I had heard this story before. Kat had warned me about this. "Your mother tried to claim rape and your father snapped."

That was a lie. Kat never said she claimed rape. One thing about Kat, everything she was and everything she did, she owned. I remember her telling me one day, *If you big enough to do it, be big enough to own it*. She made no apologies for who she was. She never tried to play victim either. All those long walks to the shelter when I was five, right before I went to live with Big mom, I remember them. Those long walks were filled with Kat telling me about her and her life. At five years old, they were just words but her voice was embedded in my head so when I was old enough, I recalled them and made sense of our talks. It was like a jig saw puzzle, bits and pieces from Aunt Bobbie and bits and pieces from Aunt Debbie and now Carmen and the one piece that made it all make sense was Kat's.

My mother was the black sheep of the family. Her mother's boyfriend raped her and her mother died never acknowledging it. Kat was fucked up from that. She never recovered. Her life was all down hill from there. I think she was doomed from birth though being as though her mother was a drunk, her father was murdered in front of her. That and she was the baby, all of her siblings having different fathers, none who stayed around to help my grandmother raise their children. Kat followed in her mother's footsteps having children by multiple men, having an addiction, never being held accountable. It was a vicious cycle. Wouldn't be me. But everybody saw Kat when they saw me and the Washington's saw Kitty, the woman who destroyed their family and murdered their brother, and son. I was the black sheep of my family, constantly punished for things I had nothing to do with.

I could feel my Aunt Carmen's eyes on me whenever I'd look away. I could tell she saw Kitty when she looked in my eyes. She always sucked her teeth, cut her eyes, and turned her lips up in the air when I would be talking.

I wanted to believe that she wasn't like the rest of them because she was just a child when all the mess with Kat had happened. When we didn't talk about Kat or Desmond she seemed like she genuinely was there for me. She was really young, not even thirty and her daughter Safiyah was only a year younger than me. My Aunt had four children.

"You should be so grateful for us. We saved you. That damn Kitty sold you for crack when you was barely a month old. My mom had to go get you from those white folks. They wanted a baby so bad, they paid two thousand dollars cash for a black *baby doll*. That's what they said they wanted."

I hit the mite button in my head.

We went to pick up my thing that evening from Cash's house. Cash was acting like she was so sorry for being an asshole. I wasn't buying it. I stopped at my Aunt Debbie's house where my Aunt Carmen and Aunt Debbie needed to have a "private" conversation.

Once we were back in the car my Aunt Carmen blurted out "Your family full of shit. They always have been and always will be."

I leaned back in the seat and put my seatbelt on and prepared for the long ride.

It was a long ride but my stay at Aunt Carmen's was short lived. Five months to be exact. The constant fighting and arguing with Safiyah was driving me crazy. I would stay at Keisha's house on the weekends just so I could avoid being around Safiyah..

Safiyah and I got into a huge fight one day and I left. I went to Keisha's and stayed for a week. Aunt Carmen was heated. She worked three jobs and was never home. I barely saw her. I told her that I would come back when she came home. Safiyah had worn my clothes without asking and ruined a pair of my hundred dollar jeans. My perfume was running low and my diamond studs that Kareem had brought me went missing.

When I finally went home, my clothes were all packed up in trash bags. It was just three days after Christmas. I called my Aunt Carmen at work and she said, "Azhar, this isn't working. You have to leave." I hung up the phone before she said anything else. I sat on the edge of the couch and Safiyah came barging through the front door. She was all sweaty and clearly had been crying.

"Yo, something real bad just happened! You talk to D-Dot?" She paced the floor trying to catch her breath.

"No, why?"

"Yo, it was a bad shooting down the bottom."

"It's always shootings down the bottom." I sat the phone down. It rang immediately. "Hello."

"Let me speak to Safiyah." The voice barked. It was one of Safiyah's little friends. I gave her the phone.

D-Dot was this guy I had met one night I went down the bottom with Safiyah. The bottom was what we called the bottom part of West Philly. It was the end of the summer and I had on some cute white shorts, a white wife beater and my hair pulled into a ponytail with a bun on top. I was standing on the corner talking and this guy walks over with a water ice in his hand, smiling. He introduces his self to me as D-Dot.

"I'm Azhar." I greeted him. He wasn't light skinned so I wasn't really checkin for him. But he was nice, and drove me home that night when Safiyah decided she wanted to spend the night at her boyfriend house. D-Dot was a street nigga. According to Safiyah he was "getting money." I didn't care about that though. I liked that he was checkin for me hard. He would pop-up at my Aunt Carmen's house unannounced, blasting his music in his white sports car. He would drive me to school some mornings and take me uptown on the weekends to stay at Keisha's. D-Dot would always tell me how he wanted to "just graduate and join the Marines." I had never heard anyone say they wanted to join the Marines. D-Dot didn't act nothing like the street nigga he showed everybody else.

In the five months that I knew D-Dot, we never had sex. We hung out at the movies, downtown and sometimes down the bottom where he hustled at. I didn't like going down the bottom because no matter what I wore or how I did my hair, I always stuck out and everybody could tell that I wasn't from down there. When I would tell them I was from Uptown they always have something slick to say.

"What?! Oh my goodness! Don't play like that!" Safiyah slammed her hand down on the kitchen table. "Oh my God no!"

"What's wrong?" I jumped to my feet. "What's wrong Safiyah?"

76

Safiyah dropped the phone. She sat down on a crate that was near the window.

"Somebody killed D-Dot. They shot up the whole stash house." Safiyah cried out, placing her head in her hands.

I was speechless. Safiyah had known D-Dot for years. She was so happy when she found out we were seeing each other. She looked at him like a brother. He was well known. My Aunt Carmen even knew him. His family was big and well known for running things down the bottom. I held Safiyah as she cried. The phone rang, jerking us both back to the present.

I left that night. All of Safiyah's friends kept calling and my Aunt Carmen even came home from work early. The Lex Street Massacre, that's what the news was calling it. It was on every news channel. When I finally made it to Keisha's house in the cab that night, my heart was so heavy. Keisha helped me drag my four trash bags of clothes and two duffle bags into her house.

Upstairs I sat on Keisha's king size bed. "I don't know where I'm going to go."

"I'll ask my mom if you can stay here with us. She's never here anyway." Keisha picked up the phone and dialed. "Mom, can Azhar stay here with us? Her Aunt put her out." Keisha passed me the phone.

"Hello."

"Hi Azhar, what's going on? Where's your mom?"

I thought for a second. I didn't know how to answer that question. Was she referring to Kat or Debbie. "Um, my mom?" My heart beat began to pick up. I didn't want to have this conversation. "Well, my mom, my mom is." Tears burst out my eyes full force. *Where the fuck was my mom*, I thought. "I don't have a mom. I don't have a dad, or anyone." I confessed in between loud sobs.

"Yes you do Azhar. Where is your mom? Everyone has parents."

"I don't know where my mom is." I cried harder, barely able to speak.

Keisha grabbed the phone. "Mom, I told you her mom is on drugs. She doesn't know where her father is! Can she just stay here? She can have my room and I'll sleep in the guest room."

Keisha's mom didn't agree to me staying there. She did allow me to stay the night though. That night I confided in Keisha about Kat having HIV. She cried. I cried. We sat up all night long talking. I told her about D-Dot and I cried more. My heart hurt so badly that night. Keisha was speechless.

"Azhar, why would you keep this stuff from me? You don't look like all of this stuff."

"What do I look like then?" I was curious.

Keisha laughed, lightening the mood. "A fierce bitch!" We both bust out laughing.

CHAPTER 12

The next morning I called a number that Cash had given me for Kat. Cash said Kat was clean and had an apartment here in the city. The phone rang four times before someone picked up.

"Hello." It was a man's voice.

"Hello may I speak to my mom?"

"Who is your mom?"

"Katherine!"

"Who is calling?"

"Her daughter." I sucked my teeth. *Clearly*! I heard some shuffling sounds and then Kat's voice.

"Hello." It was like music. A fine, soothing tone.

"Mom."

"Who is this? Zhar?"

"Yes mom, it's me."

Our tones were low, even. Long pauses between our words gave us both time to think. I had never called Kat before. Not for anything.

"What's wrong?" Panic spiked in her voice.

"I'm okay. Nothing is wrong." I tried to calm her. I was lying. Everything was wrong. My entire life was a mess. I didn't know if I was coming or going. My days ran into nights and I was changing my address as much as I was changing my panties, it seemed. I was fighting daily in school but now I was smart enough to wait until school let out so that I wouldn't get suspended. But still, I was fighting. The fights were growing into full fledged riots which would start as my crew and I jumping someone to fifty and sixty people being involved simply because they knew us. We were fighting other kids from other schools on the buses, on the trains, anywhere. I carried mace and an icepick and wasn't afraid to use it. Because of all the fights I was in, I didn't travel alone anywhere. We all traveled in a pack, at least fifteen deep. We went downtown, to movies, to the doctors, everywhere together.

"Okay baby, you sure?"

"Yes mom. I just was calling because Aunt Carmen put me out and I don't have anywhere to stay."

"What? Why were you at Carmen's anyway?"

I gave a short story about all the moves I had over the past year or so since the last time I had heard from her. She gave me her address which was five minutes away from Keisha's. I called a cab and took my things around to her house, not even thinking twice.

It was a duplex apartment. The first floor. It was filthy dirty. It looked abandoned, like Kat was squatting instead of renting. In the living was a hospital bed where a man lay under several blankets. Kat led me to the back room where the windows were boarded up and a fog light hung from a closet door.

Kat had cut all her hair off. It use to hang down her back but now it was so short I could see her scalp. It looked good on her thin face but different.

"Who's house is this mom?" A twin mattress lay in the middle of the wooden floor with a sheet thrown on it with obvious stains.

"This is Mister's house."

"Who?"

"Mister." She repeated again in the same even tone as before. One thing about Kat was, she never indulged with my sassiness. My slick mouth would be going and she would hold her composure. When we was out Michigan and I got all flip lip with her, she didn't even yell at me. She bent down so that we were eye to eye and she spoke slowly and sternly. She always reminded me of who was the child and who was the adult.

"Who is that?" I continued but cautiously as to not allow my disgust show so boldly.

"My friend. When he gets up I will introduce you to him." Kat moved a dresser from one side of the room to the other. She opened each draw and closed them back. "You can put your things in here. It's not all fancy like you're use to but, just wipe it down and it will be good as new."

I looked around the gloomy room. It was dusty and I tried to imagine waking up in this old box, because that's what it felt like. After I wiped down the dressers, I caught the bus to the mall to get some sheets, a blanket, tooth brush, soap, and other daily living essentials of my own. When I walked in Kat was sitting on a crate with a little table in front of her smoking a cigarette. Mister was sitting up on the edge of the bed. I didn't understand why it was in the living room. As I got closer and adjusted my eyes from the outside light, I could see Mister clearly. His face appeared to be drooping, he was extremely thin, frail, like he was sick or very old.

"Hello Azhar."

"Hi." I waved. I stood behind Kat.

"Your mom has told me so many great things about you. I'm sorry we couldn't have been there for you to keep you from going through some of the things you went through, but." He paused to catch his breath. He began to cough. The cough grew out of control into a bark. Kat jumped to her feet and offered him a bottle of water that sat by his bed. I took this time to retreat to the bathroom. The small bathroom reminded me of a public rest room so I treated it as such. I lined the toilet with tissue and did my best not to touch anything. I pulled back the shower curtain out of curiosity. The tub was pilling paint and rusted around the drain. I cringed. I went to the space Kat referred to as my room and paced the floor.

God, please help me. This cannot be my life. A tear tried to escape my eye but I forced it away. Now was not the time for tears. Kat appeared in the door way.

"Baby girl, let's talk." She plopped down on the mattress that I had not yet put new sheets on. She patted the space beside her for me to sit. "You're becoming your Aunt's child." She said. My facial expression must have told her that I was not going to sit on that bed.

"Mom."

"Azhar, we've lived in worse places than this." She had a point, I suppose but I was a child and didn't know any better. There was no way I was going to sit on that bed. I pulled myself up on the dresser and folded my legs in Indian style.

"Wassup?"

"You can stay here as long as you want. Whatever I have is yours. It's not much." Kat explained. "But, it's all I have." Her eyes were soft with empathy.

"I won't be here long. I'm going to get an apartment with Keisha." Keisha and I had came up with that plan the night before.

"Azhar how old are you, fifteen, sixteen?" She said, amused.

"Sixteen!" I corrected her. "I'm sixteen mom." *All the drugs must have fried her brain! She can't even remember how old her own child is.*

"Azhar, I know you're all independent and whatnot but that's just too young to be living on your own. You can stay here until you graduate school."

"I just need a few months. Keisha and I are going to get a two bedroom apartment. I've basically been raising myself for the past two years anyway."

Kat didn't look convinced. "Okay Azhar. I know I can't stop you."

She was right about that. At this point I was trying to figure out how I could get emancipated. Nobody wanted me so I didn't want nobody tryna tell me what to do whenever they felt like dropping back into my life. Keisha and I had planned it all out. Keisha was already seventeen and would be eighteen soon so she would sign for the apartment and be my guardian on paper.

"There's something else I need to talk to you about." She locked her eyes in with mine as I tried not to roll my eyes.

"What?" *What else could possibly be wrong now?* I thought.

"Mister is sick."

"Obvious. What he had a stroke or something." Kat attracted what she was. All her men were drugs addicts, unstable and none stayed around long enough to ever marry her lie they all promised.

'Come on Azhar. Don't be like that."

"What?" I snapped back.

"He has AIDS."

Someone punched me in the throat. All the air had been sucked out of me. *Breathe.* I reminded myself as I felt myself getting dizzy sitting up on that dresser.

"What?! Are you crazy? Aren't you already sick? What's wrong with you?" I blurted out.

Kat's eyes magnified. We had never had a conversation about her being sick. When I was in Michigan we had a big argument about me not wanting her to touch me. She tried to explain to me that I couldn't catch HIV by touching her but I was not hearing her. "I just want to hug my daughter." She cried to me. I hit the mute button in my mind and blocked her out. *She did this to herself*, I repeated over and over to myself.

"Azhar you don't understand. I have HIV-"

"HIV, AIDS, what difference does it make? You're sick and dying and he's more sick and dying!" The adrenaline was flowing through my body. I jumped down off the dresser to my feet. "Why'd you have to do this to me? Why'd you have to ruin my life? I never asked to be here! I didn't ever want to be born. I wish I was dead. Please God take me away!" I screamed as I no longer could contain the tears. I ran through the kitchen and out the front door.

The cold air hit my face full force. I walked to the corner and put a quarter in the payphone. I dialed Rahiem's number. There was no answer. I hung up before the answering machine came on and the phone took my quarter. I dialed Kareem's pager and put the payphone number in with my code 333 behind it. I was freezing but I told myself if Kareem didn't call back in three minutes I would go to Keisha's house.

The phone rung back immediately. "Hello."

"Wassup shorty?"

"Can you come get me? It's an emergency."

"Wassup? I'm on the road baby girl."

"it's a lot. I need a place to stay for the night. I'm looking for an apartment too."

"You got some coins on you? I can get you a room at the Double Tree for the night. I just gotta call my man. He'll meet you at the hotel and book the room."

"I'm on the corner of Broad Street." I masked my pain and tears. I told Kareem where I was and waited for his friend Sean to pick me up. I dipped into the Chinese store to shield myself from the forty degrees temperature.

A half hour later Sean pulled up in a white Benz. The seats were midnight black, leather. The car smelled amazing.

"Wassup?" Sean nodded his head.

"Hey." I had never met Sean in person before but Kareem always talked about him. Whenever Kareem needed something done, he's call Sean.

"So you're Azhar? The beautiful and intelligent Azhar." He smiled, showing his chipped tooth. His full beard was neatly groomed and his bald head was shinny. He looked me over as if she was trying to figure out a puzzle or something. "Where's your coat at shorty? Kinda cold out here, ya dig?"

"It's a long story."

"When people say that, they usually mean they don't wanna talk about it."

"Yup."

"That's cool. How bout we shoot to the mall real quick and grab you one. Kareem said to take care you." He looked straight ahead and began to drive.

"That's cool."

"You don't look sixteen yo. I can see how Kareem could easily forget that."

Speak less, listen more. People always show their intentions. I could hear Kareem's voice in my head. "Hmp."

"Yeah, so, you staying at the hotel tonight?"

I turned my head to look at him. He was smiling. He turned to look at me. I let my facial expression go blank. The rest of the ride to the mall I just zoned out. I kept visioning Kat's face in my head. She looked so hurt. But how could she be? I was the one who was hurt. I was the one who was constantly paying for her and Desmond's fuck ups.

That night at the hotel I didn't call anyone. I didn't return any of the six pages that I got from Kareem or the two from Keisha or the one from Rahiem. I showered and ordered room service. While I waited for the food I took out a fresh note book I picked up from CVS on the way to the hotel. Sean didn't bother me much after I ignored him the first two times he tried to pick me for information.

Dear Diary,

They killed D-Dot. I can't believe it. I never experienced death before. It's all over the news. They say this is the biggest mass murder in Philadelphia's history. They tryn'a say D-Dot was this big time drug dealer. I guess that's the perception everybody had on him. Nobody knew he still was a pizza delivery guy too. Nobody knew he wanted to get out the hood and join the Marines. They saw his flashy car and thought the worse. I admit, I did too, at first. I miss him already. I wish I could call him right now. I can't call anyone right now. I don't have anyone. I don't even think I have Rahiem anymore. I hear he's seeing some other girl. He denies it of course. I want to talk to Kareem but I don't know what to say. I don't know where to begin with all this craziness.

The next morning the sound of the phone ringing pulled me out of my sleep. "Hello."

"Baby girl, you don't see me paging you?"

"I was sleep." I sat up in the bed and tried to focus my eyes.

"Open the door."

I opened the room door to see Kareem standing there with a dozen of roses. "Roses for my beautiful baby girl." He smiled and kissed me on the cheek. My insides fluttered. I had begin to feel something for Kareem but I didn't know what to call it. When I thought about it, I always dismissed it when the thought that I could actually love him came to mind. I felt guilty. I felt like I was betraying Rahiem. Besides, every time I started feeling like this, he would go away, leaving me. He always left. Everybody always left me.

My pager began to buzz. It was a number I didn't recognize. I dialed the number back. It was Asia. Asia was little Tony's new girl girlfriend. Asia and Tony met through Leigh. I had met Asia once or twice at the shop so I was surprised that she was paging me.

"Hey Zhar."

"Hey." I said hesitantly.

"Your mom gave me your number. She's here now."

"Who Kat?"

"Yeah, you only have one mom!"

"I know but I thought you were talking about Aunt Debbie."

"No, I'm talking about the woman who birthed you. Carried you for nine months. The woman who's sitting on my couch crying her eyes out because you ran out on her."

"Man, come on Asia. Don't fall for that."

"Fall for what? I'm just saying, you don't just run away because you don't like what somebody saying to you."

"Asia, I didn't run away. I just left. I don't have to stay with Kat. She's not my mo-"

"Mom? Then what is she then?" Asia's tone had gone up a few notches.

I rolled my eyes. Kareem was looking through the menu on the dresser but I knew he was listening.

"Asia, can I call you back later?"

"No, you can bring your behind to my house immediately so you can sit down and talk to your mom. You are not grown Azhar. You are only sixteen. That's not grown!"

"Okay." I only agreed because her tone seemed serious. "Where do you live?"

"Around the corner from your mom." She gave me the address and I scribbled it down on the note pad next to the bed.

"Azhar, you're so angry with Kat you won't even hear her out. Give her a chance."

"Asia, you don't know Kat. I don't even know why I went to her. She's always been the same, a disappointment. I know she sold my clothes the minute I walked out her house!" My arms were folded in front of me because it was the only thing I could do to keep from actually swinging on Kat. She sat on Asia's couch in tears, sobbing.

"Azhar I swear I didn't steal your stuff, Mister must have taken it."

"You expect me to believe that old ass, crippled, man who barely could sit-up stole all my clothes, all my shoes and my damn money?! Do I look like a damn fool to you? Do you remember I know you use to steal Aunt Bobbie's stuff too?" I paced back and forth. "I'm your daughter! How could you do this to me?"

"Azhar, calm down and stop cursing. Respect your mother." Asia interjected.

"Respect? Does it look like she respects her damn self?" I screamed. My blood was boiling with each passing thought. I had taken my last five hundred dollars out my account because I was going to buy a new bed. I figured if I had to stay in that box, the least I could do was have a clean place the sleep. I ran out of Kat's house so fast I forgot to grab my pocketbook. I had nothing. All my stuff was gone. I had the one outfit on my back and the one I had worn the day before to the hotel. I couldn't ask Kareem for anymore money. He jokingly had said I was over my monthly allowance of six hundred dollars. He had brought me the diamond studs for my sixteenth birthday and I had yet to tell him that Safiyah had stole them.

"Azhar, I would never steal from you." Kat said. I cut my eyes so hard at her. I wanted her to stop talking to me. I wanted her to leave, to go away like she always did. Why was she here anyway?

"You know what, I don't care. I'm not mad. How can I even be mad? All the shit you have done to me, to Cash, to yourself? How the hell can I even be mad at you?" I took a deep breath and sat on the couch across from Kat.

That day after Kat left, I sat on the couch and talked to Asia. Again, I was telling my story of how I had ended up on her couch.

"Azhar, once you become one with who you are, nobody can tell you shit. Own who you are. Own your story, allow the pain to push you!" Asia held me in her arms like her own child. She held me for what seemed like hours. I talked, she listened. She talked, I listened. I told her about everything. About Rahiem, Kareem, D-Dot, all the other guys that were coming at me left and right and how I felt overwhelmed with it all. I told her about Nikki and how she had completely cut me off and how Leigh use to be my hero until she met Mike. I told her about the FBI but none of this was a surprise because lil Tony had already told her.

"You're going to be alright Azhar. You're going to get through this. I know you are. You're strong. I can see that." Every day Asia reminded me of how strong I was. She kept telling me that I was special, a fighter, a survivor. She took me to the book store and brought me a bible and I got to choose one book I wanted. I chose *The Coldest Winter Ever*.

I finished out the school year strong with the help of Asia. She was a stay at home mom to her three children and kept on me about my grades. When I came home from school, she would make me sit at the dinning room table and do my homework before I could hang out with Keisha.

Things were, okay. Kat visited often, never allowing me to fully escape like I wanted to.

CHAPTER 13

Imhotep. The summer of my eleventh grade of high school, I decided to transfer to a small Charter school that recently opened not too far from where I was living with Asia. This would be my third and hopefully, final high-school. I knew nothing about the little school that operated out of eleven small trailers on a once vacant lot. I did however, know the neighborhood. The school was one block from where I spent the first eleven years of my life, living with my Aunt Bobbie.

Imhotep was a small, family oriented school where everyone knew everyone. It felt like home. The teachers were on the younger side and all looked like me. Imhotep was an African Centered Charter school that placed emphasis on educating the youth about their culture and heritage as it pertained to being the descendants of Africans. We addressed our teachers by Bobba, Brother and Sister. We wore colorful dashikis and began each day at 10 am with our Affirmation Statement:

We are descendants of
Great African Fathers
And
Great African Mothers.
We will have the pride, strength
And power of the motherland.
To help us do the things we must
Do
Because we must understand
I am because we are and we are
Because I am
When I shine the nation shines.
And when the nation shines we all Shine.
Hotep!

I had never heard these words before. I had never thought about myself as a Queen before walking through the gates of Imhotep, but all of my teachers always addressed me as such and when I wasn't acting in accord, they would remind me of who they thought I was, Queen. School for me, again, was an escape. An escape from reality. Any thoughts of my real life were placed on hold until 5:00pm when the bell rang.

Life was happening so fast for me and things were always changing. Nothing was constant in my life, except Rahiem. I began to just accept that, nobody was ever going to save me, because they were all too busy trying to save themselves. I begin to accept that pity was not something I wanted, nor needed and if I wanted a hero, I was going to have to be that for myself. I was no longer waiting to wake up from this awful nightmare.

I worked two jobs in my twelfth grade year. I did that for about two months before I was dealt another blow.

"Miss Washington, your test was positive." The heavy set nurse said, not even looking up at me from her paper that she was scribbling on.

"Pregnant?"

"Yes dear. Pregnant."

I called Rahiem from the pay phone at the corner. "Rahiem, I had a positive pregnancy test." I felt like them. Like the rest of the girls my age who were getting knocked up by these guys and having no real education, direction or plan for their future. This couldn't be my life. I wouldn't allow myself to end up living in some Section-8 house, surviving off of Public Assistance, struggling to get a minimum wage job as some fake nurse.

"Okay, Azhar. It's okay." Rahiem was calm. This was typical Rahiem. Never flustered or moved by anything. My next call was to Keisha.

"Well if you aren't that far, schedule an appointment at Planned Parenthood." As always Keshia had the solution to every problem imaginable. "It's not the end of the world Azhar."

I skipped school that day and headed straight home to talk to Asia. She was lying across the couch when I entered the house.

"What are you doing home?"

I handed her the slip the doctor gave me that said I was eight weeks pregnant based on my last menstrual cycle.

"Aw, Azhar. What happened to the depo?" Asia's tone was subtle and comforting. I had expected her to yell, be mad and ultimately kick me out. She didn't though. She talked to me about my options and I told her that I didn't want any children ever, but that I was scared to get an abortion.

"You can get put to sleep Azhar. You don't have to be woke during the procedure."

I called and scheduled my appointment for the following week. Rahiem was not happy about my decision. He wanted me to keep the baby. I told him that wasn't an option because I was going away to college.

"Azhar Washington." The young female called from behind the desk.

The waiting area was jammed packed with other pregnant females, waiting to have the lives sucked out of them too. Asia told me the day I found out that I was pregnant not to think about the life in me as "my baby" because I would get emotionally attached, so I didn't. Rahiem kept trying to convince me to change my mind but I wasn't trying to hear anything about moving in with him and his mother in a crammed two bedroom apartment, and I was sure Asia wasn't going to allow me to bring another mouth into her already crowded home. Besides, I didn't even like kids. Leigh had used up all my patience when it came to children. I had been watching her brats since I was eleven years old. I absolutely did not want any children-ever. I was going to go to college for a year or so and then move to New York and become an actress or print model. Maybe I would be a writer or professional ballet dancer. Anything. I was going to be anything but a teen mom or some other statistic.

"Azhar, count backwards from twenty." The tall, thin white man instructed.

I closed my eyes and began praying instead of counting. "Please God forgive me for my sins. Please God keep me in your arms. Please God. Forgive me." A vacuum noise filled the air. I tried to open my eyes but my eyelids were too heavy.

"You are beautiful! When you were first born, you came out with a head full of hair and it was perfectly wrapped around your head as if you had went to hair salon." Kat stroked my hair as I lay in her lap. Her clothes smelled musty and stale. I could detect cigarettes all on her fingers too but I didn't care because it felt so good to hear her voice and see her eyes light up as she told me stories about my childhood.

"Mom, are you going to stay this time?" The words barely escaped before I began to feel the lump swelling up in my throat. I was fighting back the tears with everything in me.

"You know Azhar, I have to just run and meet my friend real quick and I'll be right back. I'm gonna stay this time just for you, okay. I just gotta go get this money real quick."

Kat hopped up and hurried right out the front door. I sat there at the screen door for hours waiting for her to come back. I didn't sit, or move to use the bathroom, or even eat. I stood there until my little eight year old feet couldn't bare my weight anymore. It was pitch dark outside but I was determined to wait for Kat to come back and stay, like she said.
She never did.

"Would you like some crackers?" A lady wearing scrubs asked as she stood above me. I wasn't quite sure where I was. I looked from side to side. I was sitting in a recliner chair and on both sides of me set other females. Both black, seemingly young girls.

"Where am I?" My mouth was dry. So dry the sound barely escaped.

"You're in the recovery room. You just had a procedure done. Would you like some crackers with your juice? Take the crackers. It will help with the nausea feeling."

Before I could respond she placed three packs of saltine crackers on the small table beside me. The girl to my left was reading a magazine. I was still trying to gather my thoughts and like that, I remembered. Abortion. I had just gotten an abortion. My first reaction was to look down as my belly. I unconsciously rubbed it. Was it gone? I looked to the right of me, my eyes met with another girl in sneakers and grey sweatpants.

"This your first time?" She quizzed.

I didn't know if my face was inviting or not but I wasn't in the mood to sit and chat it up like I hadn't just killed a life. My eyes scanned the room. Twenty. There were twenty of us sitting in recovery. Twenty babies had just been killed.

"This not my first one. It's my third." Miss Prada sneakers admitted without me questioning. I guess she was just going to force this conversation no matter if I wanted to partake or not.

Once home, I climbed into Asia's king sized bed like a seven year old little kid, instead of the seventeen year old teenager I was and I began to write until my eyelids collapsed.

Dear Diary,

I did it. I got an abortion. Rahiem is so mad at me but then, I am so mad at him too, so we are even. He's still doing him. I know he is. Asia's sister told me she saw him driving my car on Chelten Ave with some light skin girl in it. He swears it was his mom though. I don't believe him. I just want to get through these next six months of school. I promised Asia no more fighting or arguing with other girls about Rahiem. Honestly, it's exhausting trying to police him and fighting with them, working and going to school. I'm so drained. Kat came over the other day, she's looking good. She cut all her hair off again. She's thirty five days clean she said. This is her second attempt this year. Of course she blamed me for her leaving the good one year program that Asia had found her earlier this year. She said she was mad that I wouldn't come see her during visitation day. She must have forgotten how many times she didn't come see me throughout the years when I needed her and I didn't go giving up on life or dropping out of school or something.

CHAPTER 14

It was a Thursday morning, the house was silent. My two way pager had woke me up. It was Kareem saying *Congratulations baby girl*. His message brought a smile to my face. I hadn't seen him in months but he always sent me a text to let me know he was thinking about me. He kept his word. He paid my pager bill monthly and sent me money every now and again. The four hundred dollars that he had sent me this month went to the Black strappy Fendi sandals I was about to sink my feet into and strut across the stage and get my piece of paper.

I sent Keisha a text, *you ready? lets go do this bitch*! I was so excited I barely slept the night before. By the time I had dressed, checked myself in the mirror a thousand times, I heard Leigh coming down the hall.

"Good morning."

"Hey, good morning." I replied fixing the diamond tennis bracelets that laced my arm.

"What time does it start?"

"Ten o'clock. I left the tickets on the table downstairs."

"Killin 'em in those sandals." Leigh gushed, bending down a bit to get a closer look. "Damn Azhar, you doing okay for yourself." Leigh stood behind me and fixed what appeared to be some out of place strands of hair. My silence must had sent smoke signals to Leigh. "Why so quiet? Aren't you excited?" She smoothed my hair down with her hands and gave a final pat on my head. "Much better."

"I am excited." I forced a smile. In my head I ran through happy images to force back the tears that were trying to form. Today was bitter sweet. There I stood in my little black BCBG dress, in my five hundred dollar Fendi sandals, two twenty-four caret white gold tennis bracelets, two caret matching earrings, and a Prada clutch, all that I had just pulled out of two green trash bags. *Pretty good for a crack baby born in the slum of Richard Allen*

90

Projects-I guess. I smirked at the thought.

The trunk of my car was still jammed packed with most of my stuff since Shay had put me out. I was tired of packing and unpacking, to pack and then unpack again. I told myself that I would just leave my stuff in my car until I went away to school. Asia's abrupt departure still didn't sit well with me. When she decided to up and move to Atlanta, my entire world fell apart. I had only lived with Asia for a little over a year. My eighth move since ninth grade. The summer of my eleventh grade year when I found myself sitting on her couch crying my eyes out to her, I had no idea she would come into my life and help me grow into the women I saw standing in the mirror the morning of my high-school graduation. Asia's family took me in like their own. Her mother and her sister Shay. Asia saved me. She saved me from myself and what I thought I wanted, which was to be a Jones. But there I stood, back at the Jones's house because just two days prior, Shay had walked in on me having sex with this guy name Tay on her couch. She was too through. She packed my stuff while I was at work. Leigh agreed that I could come back "home" since I was about to go away to school in a few weeks.

So as I stood there looking at my reflection in the mirror, my big brown eyes piercing back at me, for the first time ever I saw myself and I wished that Asia was standing there and could see me too. Instead, Leigh was standing there with a hug smile on her face looking all proud.

"I have to go. I'll be late." I grabbed my car keys and walked down the hall, my five inch heals click clocking behind me.

The drive was rather short. I found parking and gathered my cap and gown from the back seat of my car. Inside, the entire class of 2001 gathered around to listen to instructions for the day. Keisha came over to me wearing the biggest smile ever. She was so excited. Our entire twelfth grade year, she barely passed and relied heavily on me to help her with her senior project. We both aced it, no thanks to her. It was cool though, I loved Keisha like a sister who came right out of Kat.

Keisha had taught me so much in the two years that I had known her. She wasn't all that book smart but that girl sure knew how to survive. We got jobs together, we opened up our first bank accounts together, we brought cars when we were sixteen, we went on vacations together, we did it all. Keisha showed me how to apply for credit cards and shop for bras and how to measure my cup size. She taught me about birth control, anal sex, how to douche and shave my pussy. In two years I had learned more than I did in my entire life.

Every time I had to move, Keisha was right there helping me carry those bags to my car. "Fuck ya family!" She would say. "They so jealous of you." Keisha was hell bent on my family being jealous of me. She secretly hated Nikki because she thought that Nikki was jealous of my looks. She thought Nikki was always being vindictive to me to make herself look better. The closer Keisha and I got, the more strained my relationship with Nikki got. I never even heard of family being jealous of one another until Keisha brought it up. "They always trying to make you the outcast. They just don't want to see you succeed."

I hated feeling like Keisha was right. When I moved in with Asia, she confirmed all the things that Keisha had been saying. "Your family treat you like some orphan Annie or something Azhar." Asia once said. My Aunt Debbie seemed even more angrier every time someone took me in when she would abruptly put me out. It was as if she wanted me to be homeless, out on the streets. She always had some random over the top reasoning behind putting me out. Like one time she accused me of stealing money because I was buying expensive stuff and I wouldn't tell her were I was getting the money from. And then there was a time she said I was "just out of control" because I was dating older guys. We all dated older guys. Leigh dated men old enough to be her father. They were so old we all called them Pop-Pop. Nikki dated Fats and me, I dated old guys twice my age. It wasn't like I was out looking for them. Once I turned fifteen I seemed to attract older guys. It only got worse when I brought my own car. Aunt Debbie was heated about that too. I brought it from one of my Uncle Tony's friends. She said I was too young to be driving, but Nikki got a brand new tuck when she turned sixteen. I paid for mine on my own, one thousand dollars cash. I was so proud of myself. I didn't even know how to drive or have a license but I didn't care.

Working two jobs and going to high school was no walk in the park but it felt so good to have my own money, to be able to take care of myself and not worry if anybody had forgotten about me for Christmas or my birthday. The money I made from working at the diner at nights was good. I made anywhere between four to five hundred a week. That money allowed me to pay for my college application fees and the deposit I needed to hold my room and board away at school.

As I found my spot in line and headed to the stage where all the graduates would sit, my mind drifted back over the past four years. I wondered where Kat was. I hadn't heard from her in a while. The image of her body laying dead in a crack house halted me in place. I forced it away. I thought about Asia. I missed her dearly. I thought about Cash and my two nieces. I thought about Desmond. It had been years since I last seen him. Three, maybe four. Kareem's face flashed before me. His bright smile showing his perfectly white teeth. I imagined his voice and what he would being saying to me if he were there. *Baby girl, you the shit yo! I'm proud of you.*

Kareem was my biggest cheerleader. He was so in awe with me. Everything I did, he was proud of. When I told him I got a job he was so excited for me. When I told him that I was going away to college he wanted to take me out to celebrate but I wasn't old enough to get into any clubs or drink, so we got a hotel room and ordered room service and drank Champaign. We got facials and body massages the next morning. Kareem would always say "Shorty if you weren't so young, I'd make you my girl." I never had anyone look out for me the way Kareem did with no drama associated with it. He never faked like I was his girlfriend and he never faked like he didn't know that I had a boyfriend. When we started kicking it heavy he took me out to dinner one night and said he needed to talk to me.

"We just need to establish some rules if this gone work." Kareem sat his fork down and folded his hands in front of him while looking me dead in the face. I placed my fork on the table and gave him my undivided attention.

"I know you young baby girl, and living ya life. I know these little young niggas is on you and you enjoying it." He rubbed his hands together while smiling at me. I couldn't help but blush when he looked at me. "I'm not gone sit here and act like I expect you to halt ya life for me while I'm in these streets. I'm about dealing with reality. The reality is, you way young for me to be fuckin wit." I sat back in my seat to get more comfortable. I didn't know where the conversation was going because Kareem wasn't like any other guy I had ever dealt with. He wasn't predicable in the least bit. A street nigga with a conscious. "But, I'm feelin you heavy. I'm feelin you more than I expected. You know?" Kareem wasn't really asking a question. He paused to collect his thoughts and I sat silently. "Like, you not even seventeen but you be having me thinking I'm talking to my wife and shit." Kareem was Muslim. He lost his wife two years before he met me in a car crash. She was twenty one and they had been together since she was a teenager. Kareem didn't talk about her much but the few times he did, I could tell by his tone and the way he zoned out that her loved her and missed her. She was four months pregnant with their first child when she was killed in the car accident.

Kareem went on as we ate dinner telling me that he wanted me live my life to the fullest and not to let anybody stop me from living out my dreams, especially not no nigga. "Baby girl, when we together, we together. You can always depend on a few things from me. One, I'm always gone respect you but I demand the same respect and you gotta respect ya self. You here me?"

"Yes."

"You know I'm not always gone be in the city. I gotta move in order to eat."

"I know."

"I'm thinking about getting married because I want kids." Kareem words trailed off. His eyes stayed locked with mine. I felt like he was waiting for a reaction. I didn't give him one. "Azhar, don't go fuckin up ya life having no kids by no nothing ass nigga, you hear me?"

I smirked. "Kareem, I'm never having kids, so if you need to get married and have five wives and ten kids, then do that but it won't be with me."

"Azhar."

"Kareem."

"I love that about you." Our eyes still locked, he continued. "Your mouth so slick but not on no kid, immature shit. You know what you want and you won't let anyone deter you."

Kareem explained that he had a house out New York and an apartment in Pittsburgh with some chick that he wanted to marry. "She twenty four and got two kids. She alright. Not all super smart and driven like you, but she's disciplined in the religion. She's a good girl."

"Is that all you want? A good girl?" I chuckled. Kareem disappointed me this day. He always lectured me about not settling and having standards and here he was settling for some chick because she was "a good girl." He tried to argue with me about how I didn't understand his religion so I couldn't understand his mind set when it came to this decision.

"Everybody can't have an Azhar and I can't have you."

"You're right. I'm a rarity." I said sarcastically. "Wish everyone realized that."

"Come on Azhar. If you referring to that knuckle head little boyfriend of yours, I already told you, he too young to realize what he got. You gotta give him some time. He has to experience life some."

Kareem and I had a genuine friendship. We talked about everything. He talked about his business, how he wanted to get out, his mom and how he wanted to move her out of North Philly and I talked about Rahiem and how he constantly cheated on me, making me feel like I was never good enough. Kareem was never around long enough to know about the mayhem going on in my real life. He would ask about Nikki, I would say she was fine and I left it at that. He always tried hard to make me happy. He would send flowers to my house, pop-up at my job when he was in town and onetime he had a private chef come to his apartment and cook dinner for us. He smoked and drank while I studied and watched TV. Kareem never let me smoke. He said I was too smart and too pretty to do that "ghetto girl shit." He would be so happy when I showed him my grades. I liked that a lot about him. He cared about things that nobody ever really paid attention to even though they were important to me. Kareem was in New York with his pregnant wife during my graduation. During the school year he had promised me that he wouldn't miss my graduation but he did. He sent money and a card instead. He said he couldn't travel because his wife was high risk and he probably wouldn't see me before I went away to school.

"Azhar!" Keisha yelled bringing me back to the present moment. The room was filled with parents, family and friends.

"Wassup?"

"I see Rahiem in the crowd. Is Nikki and Leigh here?" She asked.

I scanned the crowd and found Rahiem. I searched once more for Nikki or Leigh. I didn't see them. The principal began to call the names of the graduates. "Lakeisha Thomas." Keisha's family yelled and screamed so loud. I could see her mom smiling from ear to ear.

"Azhar Washington."

Everything went silent. The room slowed down, people were moving in slow motion. Forever seemed to pass.

"Zhar, go! Hurry up." Someone called out. It was happening. I was graduating high-school, in the top five of my class. I had received seven acceptance letters to nine of the colleges I had applied to and got one full ride offer. I took that offer.

I walked to the stage. When I looked out to the audience I searched for familiar faces. I darted my attention to the section screaming and clapping the loudest, hoping it was my family but it wasn't. It was Keisha's family. Her mom Trina was smiling from ear to ear just as she had for Keisha. Just as the screaming died down and I was about to exit the stage a loud whistle sounded. The kind that someone makes when they put their two fingers in their mouth. I looked toward the area where the sound had come from.

"That's right baby girl!" The voice called out. At the very back of the room near the doors stood Kareem. His smile was priceless. My excitement leaped out in the form of tears. I took my seat next to Keisha as she helped me dry my eyes. We didn't have to say anything to one another. She understood the tears. She understood my silence. She understood my brass demeanor and the bold boundaries I set. She understood why I just wasn't interested in meeting new people or accepting new friends. We were Queens of the *You Can't Sit With Us* section in the lunchroom.

Once all the names were called and everyone had disbursed into the audience to meet their families and friends, I remained in my seat. *Thank you God. Thank you God.* The tears flowed uncontrollably. I didn't try to stop them either. I was tired of masking and suppressing, hiding in the bathroom and washing them away in the shower. I cried and cried and I didn't care who saw me. I blocked everyone out and went to my safe place in my mind. There was no dinning room table to hide under like I use to do at Aunt Bobbie's house though.

My two-way pager buzzed pulling me out of my own head. *Wouldn't have missed this for the world baby girl. The two hour drive was well worth it. Have to run. Love.*

"Congrats!" Rahiem was smiling and gave me a hug. It was an empty hug. It wasn't filled with emotion like Kareem's always were. Rahiem and I were so distant now. I didn't even think he was going to come to my graduation. We hadn't spoke since the night of my prom when I left with Tay.

"Thank you."

"Where's everybody at?" The question was piercing. I ignored it. I stopped to take pictures with Keisha and a few other people I was cool with and then I headed to my car. I didn't want to go back "home" so Rahiem and I went out to lunch instead.

"So you really gone leave me?"

"Rahiem, I'm not leaving you. I'm going to college. What's here for me?" I was annoyed that we were having this conversation again. When I told Rahiem that I going away to school, he was mad. He said he wasn't but I could tell he was. Staying in Philly was not an option for me. I didn't even have a place to live. I had burned almost every bridge I ever had to stand on but Asia had once said, "better to burn them to keep from ever having to cross back over them again anyway. More than likely they will let you down like they always do."

"We could get a place together."

I couldn't help but laugh. "And do what? Kill each other?"

"Come on Azhar. We aren't that bad."

"No, we aren't because we don't live with each other." I sipped my iced tea. "I don't have to see your cheating ways every day. The best thing I could have ever done was transfer out of Germantown. All those fights, all the trouble I got into was because of you." Rahiem sat silently. He knew I was right. I didn't know anyone when I went to Germantown but by the time I had left, everyone knew me and most of them hated me.

"It sound like you don't love me anymore."

"It feels like you never did." I admitted. I avoided looking at Rahiem. My mind kept thinking about Kareem and how good he treated me. *How come we couldn't be closer in age and why'd he have to be Muslim?* I thought. I would never convert and he would never not practice the Islamic religion.

Then, I thought about Tay, he was Muslim too. He was good guy though. I met him at Clark. The streets were chasing him though, I could tell. He was checking for me hard too. We hooked up only once though but we had built a friendship while I was at Clark. We kept in contact sometimes hung out when I wasn't working.

"How could you even say somethin' like that Azhar." Rahiem shook his head. "I ain't perfect but you know I love you."

"Then why it gotta be so hard? Why it hurt so bad?"

"What hurts Azhar?" What's hard?" Rahiem snapped.

"This! Us." I gestured with my hands to emphasize the space we were in. "Why you have to cheat on me Rahiem? Damn is pussy that important?"

"Come'on man. I'm not gone keep talkin bout this Azhar. I ain't even doin nuffin. I ain't did nothing since Lisa."

"You must think just because I don't say nothing that I don't know. I'm just tired of worrying about you." I had lost my appetite. I pushed my food aside. "Lisa, Shantay, Crissy, Shantel, Felica, Dorian. The fuckin list goes on. This is so old." The anger seeped out in every word. When Rahiem first cheated on me, it changed my life. I remember wanting to die. I remember crying for days, feeling like I just couldn't go on living. I had all kinds of thoughts going through my head. I thought I was ugly. I thought I was fat. I thought he didn't like me because I wasn't light skinned. I thought all kinds of things.

It was only when I started going to Clark that I was able to function properly, or at least better than being at Germantown. At Clark everybody loved me. I had friends, Nikki, and all the guys were on me. "Fuck Rahiem" I remember Nikki telling me one night I was crying. "He's a boy. You have grown men who want you and will treat you better." And she was right. Kareem, Maine, Vance, Corey, Amir, Lateef. But there was something about Rahiem that had a hold on me. I couldn't shake him completely. My love for him was deep. He was my first everything.

I stayed out with Rahiem until late that evening. When I pulled up to park, Nikki was sitting on the Steps with Fats. I was surprised to see him there. He had never stepped foot near our house. I guess it didn't matter anymore now that Nikki was eighteen.

Don't even ask her why she didn't come to the graduation. I told myself.

"Hey wassup?" I spoke to Fats.

"Sup wit you? Congratulations!"

"Thanks." I replied dryly.

"We have to talk." Nikki said, pulling me down to the step to sit.

"About what now?" It was always something. I didn't have nothing left in me. I was so sick and tired of the drama with Nikki and Leigh and my Aunt Debbie. I just wanted to get in my car and drive away and never look back.

"It's about Kareem." Fats said.

"He had the baby, I know. I don't care." I tried to get it all out before they felt like they had something over me.

"No, not that." Nikki said softly. "He was pulled over this afternoon."

I darted my eyes back and forth between Nikki and Fats to see who was going to crack a smile first. "He got caught with a lot of bricks Azhar."

"I don't know why he was in the county to begin with."

My heart did a back flip. "He came to my graduation." The words glided out my mouth without my permission. I was talking more to myself than them anyway. I had flashed of his smile as I stood on that stage.

"What? He came to your graduation this morning?" Fats asked again.

"Yeah." I confirmed still stunned. "What are they saying?"

"It's not looking good. He had two pieces of him and had just picked up cash from a stash house."

"And the bricks." Nikki added.

"Man." Fats rubbed his bald head. "He really love you, yo."

"You say that like you can't believe it." Nikki said.

"Nah, I'm just sayin."

I left Fats and Nikki sitting on the steps. I walked pasted Leigh and my Aunt Debbie sitting on the couch. Once I got to the top of the stairs I heard Leigh say "Well, damn, hello Azhar."

CHAPTER 15

I didn't move out of bed for three days following my graduation. I didn't talk to anyone either. I called out of work sick from both jobs. Finally on the third day, I called Asia. I told her about how no one showed up to my graduation except Kareem and Rahiem and how Kareem was in jail now.

"Azhar, I think you're suffering from depression. I think you should see a doctor."

"There's nothing wrong with me. This is just my crazy life. It's fucked up. Always has been, always will be."

"Azhar don't say that. It doesn't have to be. You can change the course of your life. Look, you're going to college. The first of your mother and father's children. You have a full ride. Azhar, you are not your past. Let it go and live your life. Stop playing victim. Fuck Kat, fuck Nikki and Leigh, and Rahiem, and everything and everybody else. Fuck'em all. You're about to open a new chapter in life. Make it the best one ever."

Kiara Leon. The name on the door read. I opened the door as the hand write note on it said "come in". There was no one behind the desk, so I rang the bell on the desk. A tall, brown skinned lady appeared.

"Hello Miss Washington."

"Hello." I smiled.

"You can come on back."

The waiting are was small, only allowing for two chairs. I followed the hallway back to a larger office that was neatly decorated. The walls were grey with gold picture frames. The chairs were off white with grey circles nd gold stripes.

"I'm Ms. Leon. Sit."

I sat down on the couch. I had decided to take Asia's advice after all and talk with a therapist.

"Now, let's get right to it. Tell me why you're here?" Ms. Leon was pretty. She looked young too. She wore her natural hair pulled back in a ponytail exposing her natural beauty.

"Well, where do I begin?"

"At the beginning."

"It's a lot." I sunk further into the chair allowing myself to get comfortable.

"It usually is once people get to me." She clasped her hands together and placed them neatly over her lap. "Tell me what has transpired in the past month that has landed you here, to speak with me."

"Well, for starters, Asia left me!"

"Why did Asia leave?"

I thought she would let me tell her who Asia was first or at least ask who she was.

"Asia left because she wanted to start fresh and give her kids a better life in Atlanta. But D-Dot got killed first." I said trying to organize my thoughts. "I never got to go to his funeral and then Kat." As soon as I began to think about her the lump in my throat swelled up. I pushed her aside. I didn't want to cry. I just wanted to talk like I promised Asia I would, not cry. "Kat is my mother. She's HIV positive. Desmond is my father who killed my Uncle for having an affair with my mother. My Aunt was raising me but she used to beat the holly shit out of me and Cash. I moved with my Aunt Debbie but then we were on the run from the FBI. Shit got crazy. Leigh's boyfriend was beating her. Nikki got pregnant and carried a baby for five months but I pretended not to notice and then she secretly got an abortion. She was pregnant by a man old enough to be her father. Aunt Debbie knew but kept it a secret. I moved seven, eight, nine, I forgot how many times in the past four years." I watched Ms. Leon to see her reaction from all of this. There was none. She sat quiet with her hands folded with the same smile on her face as she had when I walked in.

"Do you mind if I write something's down?" She asked.

"No."

She grabbed a notebook and pen from her desk. "Continue."

"I thought I was suffering from depression but I don't think I am. I took a pregnancy test and I'm pregnant, again. I was just pregnant about six months ago. It's not like I don't know better because I do. I just got side tracked with all this drama in my life and I forgot to go back for my shot." I was searching Ms. Leon's face again for a reaction. Still nothing. I continued. "I think I'm pregnant by Kareem. He's looking at twenty years or something crazy like that. My Uncle Tony is in jail. He turned himself in, finally. I'm supposed to go away to college in less than two weeks. All I have to my name is a food stamp card, my car, some clothes, shoes, expensive jewelry, but no money. I have no money. All of my money I spent buying everything I would need to survive at college. I have twelve boxes of pads, eighteen tubes of toothpaste and a lot of other shit that Nikki said I would need."

"Azhar, when is the last time you took a moment to yourself?"

I thought long about the question. I didn't have an answer though. I didn't even know why the question was relevant. "I don't know. I don't know anything anymore. I don't know if I'm coming or going."

"Do you smoke?"

"No!"

"Do you drink?"

"I have before but only like special occasions."

"What about pills? Do you take pills to sleep or get high?"

"What? No! I don't do any kind of drugs. I would never be an addict."

"What do you do to cope, Azhar? How do you deal with all this mayhem and still manage to go to school, get good grades and work full-time?"

"I don't know." I shrugged my shoulders. "I don't know."

"Think about it."

"I use to cut myself." I said sarcastically to gauge her reaction.

"Use to?" She lift one eyebrow.

"Yeah. I felt like it was weak. Like I was being weak by allowing something to control me like that. That's how Kat is with drugs, Desmond is with alcohol, Leigh is with Mike, they're all weak."

"So there is nothing you do to cope?" Her question was redundant.

"No! What are you looking for me to say?" I snapped. "Rahiem? I do Rahiem! Sex. I make Rahiem have sex with me to cope." I was sitting up in my seat by now when it dawned on me. "Sex. I have sex to cope. Not just with Rahiem." My voice trailed off. Images of me having sex flashed through my head.

"Why?"

I shrugged my shoulders. "I don't know."

"How does it make you feel?" Ms. Leon stopped writing. She placed the notepad down on her desk.

"Good duh."

"Oh."

"It feels good. I feel loved."

"You feel loved. Sex makes you feel loved."

I wasn't sure if Ms. Leon was tryna be funny or not so I went with her to show her I wasn't afraid of admitting that sex made me feel good.

"Yes, I like having sex and making love. It feels like heaven. Sometimes Kareem would make love to me until I begged him to stop. Kareem always knew how to please me. He took good care of me."

"Is Kareem your boyfriend?"

"No. Rahiem is my boyfriend. Kareem is, he's." I didn't know how to answer that.

"Why isn't Kareem your boyfriend?"

"Because he's Muslim and more than ten years older than me and I'm not eighteen."

"Hmmm. And Rahiem?"

"Rahiem and I have been together since I was fourteen. He was my first. But then he started cheating and then I started cheating."

"How did that make you feel?"

I sucked my teeth. I didn't want to go down this road. "I only ever let Rahiem and Kareem make love to me. I just fucked the rest of them." I admitted.

"So you were in control? You were fucking them?"

"Yup. In this life you either doing the fuckin or you getting fucked."

"Azhar I read the journals you dropped off earlier this week like I said I would."

In that moment I felt like I was pulled back in to reality. "You did?" It was something about knowing that she had read all my personal thoughts that made me feel exposed, vulnerable.

"Yes, I did."

"And?"

"And I think you-"

"You think I'm crazy or something?"

"No." She scooted up to the edge of her seat. She looked me dead in they eye. "I think you should keep writing. I think you should keep seeing me too."

"Why?"

"Because, you need an outlet. You need an escape, a healthy one."

"So you don't think I'm crazy?" A tear slid down my cheek.

"No, Azhar I do not think you're crazy at all. I think you have been through hell and back all by yourself and you are at your breaking point." She reached her hand out and touched my knee. "You haven't broken yet which is very surprising but I think that's because at someone point in your life, I believe you suffered from DID."

"What's that? Something Kat gave from doing drugs while she was pregnant?"

She laughed a bit and patted my knee. "No. No, DID stands for Dissociative Identity Disorder. It's a disorder thought to be an effect of severe trauma during early childhood caused by extreme, repetitive, sexual or emotional abuse." She began to rub my knee again. "I read your journals and I think the abuse, both physical and emotional that you endured living with your Aunt Bobbie amongst other things throughout your childhood is the cause for it."

I sat silently trying to process her words so I kept replaying them over and over in my head.

"Is that like bi-polar disorder or something?"

"It's very complex. I'm not diagnosing you with DID. I'm just saying that I notice that you display a good amount of symptoms. Your childhood is very, traumatic." Ms. Leon stood and walked to the front of her desk. "You are an exceptional young lady Azhar. Coming from your background, I can't say that I'd expect you to be sitting here. I wouldn't expect you to be on your way to college either. Things like the things you have experienced break people early on. They typically turn to drugs or alcohol, prostitution, gambling, or something else to help them cope. You Azhar, you turned to love which you interpret as sex." She pulled my journals out of her desk. "That's not all that bad. We all need love. You just have to reprogram yourself to know that there is a difference between love and sex and one does not always equate to the other."

"Love, sex. They both feel good. I feel the best when I'm making love."

"Azhar, let's continue this conversation next week. Same time, same place?"

"Next week I have an appointment to get my procedure done."

"Okay well let's look at the following week but in the mean time, I want you to keep writing. Okay?"

I agreed.

Rahiem didn't go with me to get my procedure done. He gave me the money but he was so angry at me he wouldn't even look at me. I don't understand why he wanted me to have a baby so damn bad. Nothing about having children interested me. Not in the least bit. Every since I saw Dr. Leon and I talked to Asia, I was more excited about going to college. My full ride to Delaware State was the best thing that could have ever happened to me. None of my friends were going away to college. Most of them had jobs already and the rest were still trying to figure out what they were going to do. The morning I was leaving for school Asia convinced me to go say good bye to Kat. She said she had been talking to her on the phone for the past few days. I told her I would.

I placed the last of my stuff in my car and grabbed the mail that was on the table addressed to me. Only my first name was written on the envelope. I tore it open.

Hey Baby Girl,

I'm booked, I know you know that by now. I can't get into all the details and whatnot right now. I hope you get this letter before you go away to school. I guess now is as good as ever to express a lot of things to you. Azhar, you are probably one of the most beautiful people I know on earth. Your spirit is beautiful. When I look at you I see a woman, like you've been here before. Every time I'm around you, you make me want to be better. I always battle with myself because I know it's wrong to see you because of your age but, Allah knows my heart for you is pure. I love you Azhar. I love everything about you. I love how strong you are, how you hold it all in and all together. I see the pain you keep locked behind your eyes. I've heard the stories from Nikki too. I know about your mom. Don't be mad at Nikki. Azhar, you're so strong. I wish you would have talked to me about the things you were going through. I'm sure your side of things are way different than Nikki's, especially about you stealing. I know you would never do that. That was one of the reason's I started giving you more money. I didn't want you to want for anything. I know I can't be there for you right now and I know you probably really need someone too. But I know you will get through all of this. I feel like I let you down. I wish I could have been a real man to you and married you. If I could have, I would've. Believe that. Believe me when I tell you that you were and are always on my mind. Amina had the baby. A girl. I asked her to name her Azhar. She agreed. I probably will never see my daughter other than behind a glass window. I pray she is as smart and ambitious and strong as you. I know you're about to go out here into this world and hurt a lot of niggas hearts, just remember you have one too. Azhar I want to school you on so much shit about these niggas but I feel like you probably already know just because of they way you had me open and you not even legal yet. I use to try to shake you by keepin my distance. Even with Amina and Nadja, my other new wife, and at least a dozen other chicks, none of them came close to you. I was always looking for them to be as funny as you, or as smart as you, or have that sassy attitude like you but they never was on your level. I even watched Nikki sometimes to see if maybe it was genetic or something. It's not. Nikki remind me of them-shallow. Your whole thought process is just different. Keep it that way. Keep being the strong independent thinker you are. I'm not gone tell you to keep in touch and all that shit. I did this shit, this my bid I gotta do and like I always tell you, I want you to live your life to the fullest but just always know that if you need anything Azhar and I mean anything, you get wit Fats or Sean. Whatever it is, I already told them to make it happen for you. I love you with all my heart, may Allah watch over and protect you.

Kareem Abdullah.

Dear Diary,

This is it. I'm going to get in my car and drive to school. I can't wait to get away from here. I can't wait to start fresh. Kat left me, Desmond left me, Cash left me, D-Dot, Asia , and now Kareem. Everyone I ever loved- left me. Rahiem mind as well had left too. He left the day he cheated with Lisa. He broke our bond. Nikki and Leigh both turned their backs on me. I'm writing because I won't make it to see Ms. Leon.

Kareem-of all the people in the world I miss him the most. More than Kat, more than Desmond, more than anything. Ms. Leon says that it's because he was a father figure to me, that he showed me a love that I had been yearning for. She said it both good and bad. I don't know. Nothing about Kareem felt bad.

Ms. Leon told me that just because Kat has HIV, that doesn't mean she's going to die. She gave me a book on HIV and AIDS to read. I'm going to read it when I get to school. She told me that I should give Kat a big hug before I leave for school. I haven't given Kat a hug since I was eleven, that was nearly six years ago.

I finally read The Coldest Winter Ever. I get it now why Bobba kept calling me Winter. But I'm no Winter. I'm Azhar! I'm gone finish on-top. Ms. Leon asked me how I survived all of this, I told her it was simple, there was no other option.

I met this guy name Azeem the other day. He's thirty five and has a house out Delaware. He's light skinned with dreads. He has two son's. I'm supposed to go out with him once I get to school.

ABOUT THE AUTHOR

Andrea Walker is the founder of iROC, a nonprofit organization based in Philadelphia, that provides resources to the inner city community and places extreme emphasis on HIV/AIDS outreach, education and testing. The single mother resides in Philadelphia where she spends much of her time creating, living, and loving life.
Creator of #LessonsFromMyFormerSelf – a podcast about reflections on "who I was verses who I am now"
-Andrea Walker

iAmABeautifulStruggle.com
iAmAndreaWalker.com

IG @iAmABeautifulStruggle
Twitter @iAmAndreaWalker

51586310R00070

Made in the USA
Charleston, SC
26 January 2016